What's the title?　　TITLE

What's the title?   TITLE

(APOEMNOVEL)

Serge Gavronsky

chaxpress

2018

ISBN 978-1-946104-11-3

Library of Congress Cataloging-in-Publication Data

Chax Press / PO Box 162 / Victoria, TX 77902-0162

Chax Press is supported in part by the School of Arts & Sciences at the University of Houston-Victoria. We are located in the UHV Center for the Arts in downtown Victoria, Texas. We acknowledge the support of graduate and undergraduate student interns and assistants who contribute to the books we publish. Our current interns are Renee Raven and Claudia De Luna. Ann Cefola contributed expert help toward the layout of this book.

Chax books are also supported by private donors. We are thankful to all of our contributors and members.

Please see http://chax.org/support/ for more information.

to Anne-Marie
the best reader ever

Emily Dickinson: " Title divine—is mine!" (1072)

"So you think that *I am merely deceiving you…*"

Lafcadio Hearn, *Travesty*
        (NY: A New Direction Book, 1976) p. 46

THEN

"Out of the womb-wave: the novel…"

Written by (Robinson's

"Robinson Crusoe")

"I found pen and ink."
(Daniel Defoe, "Robinson Crusoe" (NY: Signal Classics, 2008) p. 66 and
287

Now, do you really believe this:

"Lol-lolling the endlessness of poetry"

Wallace Stevens, "The Auroras of autumn" (NY: Alfred A. Knopf, 1950) p. 95

"And then went down to the ship…"

Ezra Pound, "Cantos" (NY: A New Direction Books,

1983) p.3   "They sank the ship"
Lorine Niedecker (check out Louis Zukofsky's "A"'s index…) She's not there…
Ha Ha!

"The narrative

Completed through the cooperation of the reader."

Wolfgang Iser, "The Implied Reader" (Baltimore: The Johns Hopkins Press, 1978)
p.113

Paul Valéry: "Le cimetière marin" (Hope

not!…)

«Where's the new (question?»

Now, the novel...

Read below: Cathedral

RR station

                marble

Columns

Benches

Newspaper stands

       [a trickle of crumbled tickets on a dusty waiting room floor]

        "Merdre!" Someone thinks

Luggage, with blue name tags.

"He was sprinkling himself with perfume, while we were herded to the

station."

Herta Muller: "The Appointment" (NY: Henry Holt, 2010) p.173

People, old and new   others, older, older, in wheelchairs

       [Baudelaire, "Invitation au voyage ā Cythère»] Parents yell,

  (As if their children were dogs on loose leashes.)

Wheels approach.

Clutter of noises

Rain.

       Workers clean windows

       Workers sweep floors

The conductor:

       "Get your derrières to platform A!" The conductor screams:

"C'MON!" "C'MON!"

(The conductor whispers, under his breath.)

("They're always

so slow!") (Same in Bordeaux.)
                                He rues the slowness of his de-
                                crepit train

As kids look out the windows, he says:

"Look! Beautiful France

                                        Green fields

Circular, swerving waters, spray fields all well-ordered fields

                                        Sheep

Cows under trees

                                                        "A route natio-

nale"

                                                        Fingers chalk

their

names on foggy windows.

Girls play with

their braids. Faces

on windows.
                        (The conductor checks out his German-made watch)

"Eat!"

            Lots of paper, wrapped up sandwiches

                                (Everyone imagines parents, still waving.) The
conductor knows every kid's name
Eye color

Height

            One makes a paper airplane, lets it fly down the corridor.

One makes a paper ball, and throws it down the corridor.

A country road

Small towns

Small churches

The conductor, at ease, asks:

"Who likes dogs?"

"Who likes dogs?" (he repeats)

Answers a 12 yr old: "I've got a big one! We keep her on a leash, when we go
out."
Conductor:

"Soon!"

"Soon!"

"Soon

enough!" "It's perfectly evident, made en-

tirely entirely…"
"The Yale Gertrude Stein" Selections with an Introduction by Richard
Kostelanetz (New Haven:Yale UP, 1980) p.186

(He's been driving along theses
tracks: It's
his fourth trip.)

"He leadeth his train…"

"The Book of the Dead"

Translated by E. Wallis

Budge (NY: Dover Press, 2014) no page
A 12yr old girl says:

"In my English class, our teacher read us a passage from

          "The Portable Thoreau" p.232

            "Lately, Alas, I knew a Gentile Boy."
The kids are pushed off the train.

In a stern,

Nazi voice,

A guard says:

            "To the
            Barber!"

  "Turn left, walk straight

ahead."

  It's his fourth trip.
(See Robert Antelme, "L'espèce humaine" (Paris: Gallimard, 1957), for his lived-
descriptions of a Train, taking him to Buchenwald.

            A

            watch

            tower

            Armed

            guards

            Military

            uni-

            forms
A 12yr old girl, still in her school uniform, asks:

            "When do I go home? It's time for

            my bath!"

"Every narrative contains another narrative, however continuous."
Geoffrey Hartman, "Saving the Text" (Baltimore, PA. The Johns Hopkins UP,
1981) p.107

Nobody learned that, in Latin or

Greek! "Silence!"

(In silence, she repeats what her father had memorized, for a play, he would have liked to write, on Abélard and Héloise:

> "Dieu...me frappait avec justice dans la partie de mon corps qui avait péché... »

«Daddy, where's that «Partie»?

> (In 1941, 11, 400 kids were deported, killed. (Filles et Fils, La Mairie de Paris.)

See also Anne Grynberg, «Les camps de la honte, les internés juifs des camps français, 1939-1944" (Paris: Edition la découverte, 1991)

And, Nicolas Weill, La République

et les anti-Semites. PARIS GRAS-

SET.p.113. Later,
He read Le Monde, and there, he read all about Chambon-sur-Ligne, a plateau village which
Harbored, saved, a great number of Jewish kids.

10 year old boys

12 year old girls

ROUNDED UP

(Fear of
breeding?)

(En haute saison: visite: 5 euros)

(For another information, read Ingrid Galster, «Sartre et les juifs » (Paris: La Découverte, 2003)

Before his kids reached the gas chamber,

He sang them the open:

"Allonsenfantsdelapatrieieieie"

Monsieur le Maire says:

«Cocksure men do terrible
deeds»

Salman Rushdie, "Midnight Children"(NY: Penguin Books, 1991)

p.243 (He had momentarily forgotten what Jacques Lacan had

written:

"I shall show that there is no Word without a
reply."

(NY: "The Language of the Self," translated by Anthony Wilden (NY: Dell Books,
1968) p.9

He also remembered what Primo Levy had written, in his "The Perfect Table,
translated by Raymond Rosenthal (NY: Schocken Books, 1984) p. 1946

"The faces of other men were visible, wracked by sleep and dreams of other
men..."

Not to be outdone, one of the 12 yr old girls quoted a passage from Anna
Akhmatova:

"The Birds of Death are at the zenith."

"The Complete Poems of Akhmatova" (NY: Zephir Press, 1992)p. 247

(Two days

later,

The conductor ate a filet of sole. (Sea salt from L'île de

Ré.)
As he read the last page of his favorite newspaper,

"What do you know of this..."

J. Dalton Jennings, "Solomon's Arrow" (NY: Talos Press, 2015)
p 384.

He ate

A boiled potato

Talked to himself, in half a whisper:

"De

Drancy, l'étoile jaune"

He recalled what

was still a half-memorized passage:

"Jewish Resistance"

And, for example, Paris: "L'armée juive-AJ-OJC"
OJC: rganisation juive de combat, Résistance/sauvage France: 1940-1945 (Paris:
Editions Autrement, Collection Mémoire, 2002) p. 37-117

No more silence of memory.
"I am trying to describe these things, not to relive them in my present…"
Vladimir Nabokov, "Lolita" (NY: G.P. Putnam's 1956) p. 137

(He mulled over those "situations" (to use Sartre's term from "Réflexions sur

la question juive") Sleeps soundly
Weeks go by.

A dream wakes
him up

Hopefully, will this be his last trip.

("Remembrance of Things to Come.
"   (Why not?)
"Eat!"

 Sandwiches

 Ham

Saucisson from Arles (with butter.)

More ham

Orangina   without straws.

"I have, before, had occasion to remark that I never saw any of the ordinary signs of a place of Sepulture…"

Herman Melville, "Typee" (NY: Signet Classics, 1964) p.

218. Here's another quote:

Mark Twain: "I've got the good fortune, again, but I'll not let on that I know

about it." "Puud' n Head Wilson" (NY: A Signet Classic, 1964) p. 106
                            He burned his right hand, on his hot
                            potato.

"Merde!" (Ouch!)

                                            He pushes his wife off the bed,

  Picks up a fallen pillow
                            (Was that a scene from Dante's Hell?)

After de Gaulle's victorious (much questioned by London and D.C) entry into Paris,

                        Flowers strewn the streets

Girls, crying with joy:

                    "Enfin!"

                                                Kisses (Like

                                                in a newsreel)

The mayor, wearing his bleu/blanc/rouge sash, hammers a
                            Plaque on the wall, above the double RR doors.

Kids' names-   all are- nearly-silently- read.

"We knew all of them!"

        whispers a mother (a father, an aunt, a grandmother.) Lots of dabbing of
                            the eyes.
Sniffles.

Old handkerchiefs.

(In every city, a movie house)

Newsreels of returning soldiers.

(Convoys of Limos, VIPs)

"We're not alone!"

(But who's counting?)

On the left curb, the conductor stands straight, wearing his well-ironed uniform,

Remembering what, still, no one else wanted to remember, at that very moment, before some totally unexpected revelation, took to reality:

Center

stage. "Weep no more!"

"After all, all our battles…" but then he's out of

words. "Why?"

"All that blood!"

"Think of our WWI cemeteries."
"Where shall we, officially, bury them, this "Time round?"

A voice, out of a greying crowd, says:

"I've got to get to

my job!" She leaves,

Out of that maddening crowd.

Friends follow.

A try-colored French flag is lowered, above the RR

station. The mayor keeps at the head of the new

masses.
("What gall!")

If only, thinks an old man, a student band could play, right now! BUT…

Somebody whispers: "Have you ever seen how sad our willows? I can imagine
them inside Our Cemetery Grounds, bent, leaves outlived, shuffled by the wind.

                              "Dripping above our

graves..."
                         A retired lycée philosophy

professor nods.
(Thinks...   silently.)

"Did I give, all of them, a passing grade?"

"Who can remember, especially on this very Memorable Day?"

                                   On the church steps, the priest mumbles a

prayer. Women, really, this time, not all alone, whisper, reading his lips:

                                                      "Notre Père..."

(They're all so mute with sadness....

                                                Hardly a prayer

                                                can be

mouthed.)
(In a back street, where once the Gestapo chased a member of the town's so-
called Résistance, a tire blows out.)

                         A   month later

An American (you can tell by his shoes.)
                         Steps down the train steps.

Holds on to his red

carry-on. Lights a

Gauloise.
Puffs.

The smoke wiggles its way

through the air.

(Sleeping, in the cellar, covered-over by old blankets, a crushed-up doll, a baby carriage, a wig. A large photograph, duplicates remains of those reels. Nobody knew General Paton was a rabid anti-Jew.)

In fact, if an American novelist, just off the train, could tell them how he loved Paton, in films!

And there he was, riding on his preferred white horse!

He whispers: "That's

life!"

"The Grimscride's Puppets," edited by Joseph. S. Pulver (NY: Miskatonic River Press) p.37

A. "you don't
believe it"
B. "I believe you
believe it" A. "But
do you believe it?"
B. "Does it mat-
ter?"
A. "I'm asking."

(What a fucking thing to say, at this very moment!)

(Near the RR tracks, where once that train pulled out, with all those kids, with parents sniffling, and waving handkerchiefs (as they do in movies...)

The American novelist is gently edged to

the side. He can't cross the street.
The crowd's too
thick

He says to himself:

"What a picture that would make!"

(((That's the way he would cast them, in his
novel.)))

After all, after his graduation, he was hired, as a delivery boy, for the

NY DAILYTODAY.

(Sometimes, the same dream woke him up. He thought he was Clark Kent, looking out for Lois Lane, to Rescue Her from haunting dragons. And there, in a smudgy phone booth, he would strip off his Civies, and arise in his well-ironed suit.)

In his youthful dream, he remembered... so
often,

He'd be wearing a Superman movie

habit. (Maybe for Hollyween...?)

In a nearby café, men are drinking, and they remember a line of

poetry: "Gone away from crystal tombs..."
Clark Coolidge, "The Book of During" (Great Barrington, MA, 1991)
p.142

He wipes his fic-
tional nose.

He says, to the sashed-up
mayor:

"I'm an American novelist! I'm on a self-assignment! I'm researching how a small town, like yours, lived through the war!"

He thinks to himself: "What a Truth I may be stumbling

upon!" (He smiles, as if he had just drafted the first page

of his novel!) He holds on to his red carry-on.
Looks around.

Says to himself:
                        "I've got a real
inside view of all

Those parishonnnnners!"

The retired lycée philosophy teacher asks him, where did he ever get the idea of coming to this small, insignificant town?

"I read it, (he says) in the New York Times, week-end travel section, praising your town, full of meanings for its actions during the war…"

For me, that source was meaningful enough!"

"Meaningful?"
She asks.

"Before examining the deductions in
details"

Kant's "Metaphysics of experience…"(London: George Allen, & Union, 1970)
p. 271.

I found it there, in a JELLIED, meaningful column! A claim, perhaps, to keep us from asking too many questions! Actually, perhaps, to shield meaning! I mean, shielding us from it!"

"Meaning?" She asked again She asked.
"Meaning," always shields "Meaning,"
        in the name of objectivity!
   But, you should know, I'm a novelist, migrating with

Truth!"

I asked myself, how do you translate what is printed, when Truth is uninformed? I was about to say, uniformed, as the meaning of life's a lie.

I said to myself, are we only footnotes in a text of meaning?

"What is not clear is what is clear"
Laura (Riding) Jackson "The Poems of Laura Riding" (NY" Persea Books, Inc.,1980)
p.177

You could say:

"We're all micro-texts, scribbled on a tombstone, couched in   dates."

"Technicians of the Sacred"

Edited with commentaries, by Jerome Rothenberg (NY: Anchor Books, 1969)
p. 470

He turns to the retired professor of philosophy, in that town's small reality lycée: she wanted to be reassured about the real truth of the reality of

Meaning, handed down from Aristotle to the present.

"What is not clear is what is clear"
Laura (Riding) Jackson: "The Poems of Laura Riding" (NY: Persea Books, 1980)

p.177

A true and demonstrable truth, founded-initially on mathematics, and now, in

logic. The American novelist thought it useful to suggest further readings:

the Ramayana

Mao

Pascal

(Let me add other thinkers, tinkering with MEANING's meaning.)

The young, retired philosophy prof.

"What about…"   (She stumbles) (stumbles).

The novelist adds:

"Watch out for prose."

She

thought to herself:

"Should all

theory be on paper POETRY?"

In the dark room of Search, both of us opened boxes of meaning,

as if a box, actually, contained anything, but the stench of a box

of truths.

How I fought with myself!
How
I wanted to clear the cobwebs of lies!

I concluded that we were only marionettes in the lands of falsehood.

"You read me?"

She whispers to the priest:

"does that sound like some sort of a Sunday sermon?"

He smiles for an answer and then, remembering his past, says:
"That must be an artful distortion of Truth!" And

Then   (Why not center this?)

He added: "Let's not become blind servants of falsehoods."

"You,

as a former teacher,

it's about time you flex your intellectual muscles, in my Sunday...

"Truth's direction!"

"After all..."

He says: "it's all in the accuracy of translation! Check out saint Jerome!"

The novelist thinks he can recover innumerable truths, buried in a velvet underground.

She feels up to a question, since she has a superior diploma from the Ecole normale supérieure.

Others, carefully listened, but, a young boy (one of the only boys to have survived) with his elbow, nudges another, and whispers:

"Did our retired philosopher know her blouse was left open, right down to her

navel? "

"Now, we know what she was doing, under the table, with that blue chalk!"
"Do you think her eyes need hearing aids, as she talks to all of us, on and on?"

As if the old women guessed what questions he would ask them, they replied, in a near-chorus, that, during the war, they frequently wrote to Vichy, asking those authorities when their kids would be coming back.
The returned mail always came late.

With a Vichy stamp, licked on it:................   A BEAU-

TIFULENVELOPPE.

The message was always the same:

"Don't Worry!

Everything will turn out alright!"

Then, below

an elegant signature.

Two months later, we received another letter, but this time, it said all our children had all been killed, by allied bombers.

"All handkerchiefs were soaked."

"Essential Poems and Writings of Robert Desnos" translated by Mary Anne Caws (Boston: Black Widow Press, 2007) p. 235

For the American novelist, nothing remained, but to cry (René dreamt about

figuring all that in his novel.)

In his less than a meaningful vision of reality, he asked the mayor if he could introduce him to some people who had weathered the war.

He was invited to a nearby home. He

sat in In front of the fireplace.

He read dates on the wall

16
uin
40

23
uin
40

red-white-blue.

3 octobre, 1940

She so loved that date, she had circled it

2 juin 1941

"What do they all mean?" I asked.

"All those Jews, thank God!

Killed!"

Then, a big smile.
Then, she added, with a bit of ferocity in her voice:

"All Jews should have been sent back,

Somewhere!"

"All those black fury things, on their heads! All those black, silk coats! How I

wished Napoleon had beaten them at Waterloo!"

Then she continued:

"What is not clear is what is clear"

Laura (Riding) Jackson: "The Poems of Laura Riding" (NY: Perseus Books, 1980) p.177

A few months ago,
well, to be more precise,
Jean spotted boys in the shower

Who had, between their legs, something he'd never seen before.

The coach said:

"Must be Jews."

Then, a washer woman saw Rachel, Miriam, and Frieda.

They took out their yellow stars, out of the closet.

The principal said, in his stern-

est voice: "Disinfect the pool!"
Her husband said: "We've got too many Jews in France, and especially, in our schools and in the army!"

An elderly lady told me her husband had died, falling off a crane in the harbor, a crane company, owned by a Jewish company.

In half a whisper, I quoted something I couldn't forget.

In a NY Times, film revue,

A.O. Scott wrote, about a film named:

"Wild"
"plot is enemy of truth."

 A bit further on, about that same movie, he wrote a

"Montage of Memory."

(New York Times, December 3, 2014)

I agreed,
"Whole heartedly!"

Then,
I remembered what Roland Barthes had written, in his "Elements of Semiology,"
translated by Annette Lavers and Colin Smith (NY: Hill and Wang, 1967) p.78

"In those oppositions, whose relation would be in a declaration of exteriority,
the two terms are equivalent logic."

(Then, in the back of my memory: "Droll souvenirs, recited poems."

An elderly lady, whose husband had died on the field of battle, said:

"Probably, a treasonable act, from Jews all in the Resistance"

And, then, she added:

"We're not visitors from outer-space!

"We can tell a Jew, from far away."

"Disaster finally, disaster"

 Announced, in

"Essential Poems and Writings"...Ibid. (Boston: Black Widow Press, 2007) p.235

One day, a clerk from Town Hall, told us about a letter that had been written, and
delivered to our conductor,
With a stamp from Morocco.

We knew he spoke impeccable French!

The American novelist had come with gifts, from his local town's Woolworth,
for all the kids in town. Somebody told him there were almost no kids left in town.

The mayor smiled.

"I gotta translate that "Woolworth" business in its village equivalent!" And then
he added: my translator's thrill!"

Actually, for any US journalist, immediately after the war, a translation problem

became a thrill. After all, hadn't he taken a high grade seminar on Translation?
The only proper name he could
Come up with--

        "Saint Jerome, the ideological Pater of all transla-
        tors!"

"What does he want?"

He quietly walked to the playground, with faded colors on climbing equipment.

Sees a semi-

dried-out

shower.

A pool, for Tiny Kids.   Everything reminded him of his

hometown playground,

His friends,

Mothers, on benches,   on the look-

out.

(A daddy, later,
In the afternoon, after his job, after his subway ride, after sniffing something that
Smelled Good,
        ran after a kid.

(He thinks:
        "Why in the hell would she ever want two others? Must be her mother…")

A kid slips, hurts his knee.

Cries out, so loudly, anybody could hear him, and, indeed all did!

"Need any help?"

By chance, the ice-cream vendor, just outside the playground, where he sees all of his young Customers, says:

"I'll give him a free popsicle, if he, from now on, behaves real

good!"

Applause
(A mother holds on to a French edition of:

"Le guide Marabout de la future maman."

Once, daddy had saved his son,
And...
In the meantime,
checked out all the others. That same
Mother commented on the front-page blurb synopsis:

"Here's everything you got to know, if you're pregnant."
She smiled to herself.

The Table of Contents has 9 entries, and, at the bottom of that page, an Index, and a longer Bibliography.

She smiles.
Other mothers do the same.

"Please, could I bor-
row your book?
Hand me that book!"

It's, as if, for a Riverside moment, everything else had been shoved

aside. Daddy says:

"Count me in! I'll buy a mushroom-tomato sauce

for tonight's pasta."

In the rear of his memory, he remembered--in fact-- thinks of it as if it had just happened. "What a proof of memory!"

There he is, in Grenoble, as a shabby journalist-poet,

sitting on the curb, at the

Crossing of Yev

            And

            Mi-

            aux

      A TITLE.....

A local paper, in his new town, Courchevel, where the world's greatest skiers gathered for an Olympic descent.

(News from Dachau,

on page 3   "I still

can't believe it."

           Business

           before...

The novelist walks into City Hall.

             "Where you

goin?" "Even, if a reader finds the story of Finnegan's

Wake obscure..."

            John Lechte,

"Julia Kristeva" (London: and NY, 1990) p.76

      "The mayor told me he'd be here to tell me lots

of

stories about his town!"

      "Ok!

     Up the stairs."

"Turn left!"

     (He smiles, and says to himself: "not all commies are on

     the "Left!")

"Then right."
"Left again."

"Nazi officers occupied all those offices, on the

right!" How could I have found exactly what I

wanted?
The mayor takes me to the first family,

to get a straight answer, about the town, during
WW II.

I say, in my college second-year French:

"Bonjour, madame!"

(What's up, doc?)

She smiles, out of her old age, and says, in second-hand

English:

"Please,

down, Across the fire"

I did.

She asks me: "Would you I like something to drink, like a

Calvados?"

On her little cushioned fireplace seat, I see she's been read-

ing Kafka.
"The
stair-
case.

Turn Right,

Left, again."

(I think I must have read the "Castle," or was it another of his

novels?) "Tea?" she asks.

(A French Education.)

The mayor says to her, all about what he knows about me and... when he's
finished, I check out Dates on her wall, over the fireplace.

                    It could only be
                    her truth.

                         16
                         uin
                         40

                         23
                         uin
                         40

                         3 oc-
                         tobre
                         1940

                         2
                         in

                         1.

She says, looking straight at me, looking at her chalk

board, and... Says:

                    "All those dates are my favor-

ites!"

  Smiles. She knows, At least

For a
ont,

That I didn't have the slightest
idea of what they meant.

(I see those dates, and remember:...)

"David, and the art of Politics"

(Marat in his bath,

One arm hanging as low as the edge of the
bath tub. A letter in his other hand.)
I knew nobody, in that David painting, knew anything about the knife!

David, one of the toughest, during the Terror!

And, while I'm remembering everything, I ever knew about
David, I remembered what Delacroix
had written:

"He was the father of all modernism, in painting and
sculpture."

(Could you

beat that?)

"Those

dates?"

"Vichy dates!"   (She
smiled)
"All those dates clean out the slate of our beloved country!"

"All those dates are—" She added, with a gleeful smile:

"All of them shouldn't have left their

ghettoes!"

"All those furry hats!"
"Black silk coats
"Why don't they migrate baCK to some other
country? Somewhere in
A Sandy land, surrounded by Arabs!"

Once, THEN AGAIN, SHE GOES ON

Telling me about all those Jews who had taken over

our army. "Had I ever heard, about that traitor, Captain

Dreyfus?"
"All those Jews, who are our Prime Ministers, like Léon Blum, and, I can tell you,
 right away, there will still be others, after the war!"

"Long Live Pétain!"

"Long Live Vichy!"

("What about your Hollywood Polansky? Didn't he

screw a young girl?") She smiles.
(Pours herself a shot of CALVADOS.)

Smiles

"Coffee, any-

one?"

"I got some pastries in the cub board! From our best pastry maker!"
I tell her that, that morning, as I walked by your lycée, the flag was at half-mast.

"Why? » I asked.
(Serge Klarsfeld, "Le Calendrier, de la persécution des juifs en France 1940-
1944 »)

I was about to quote all those unbelievable dates.

She'd accuse me of being a Jewish Resistance jour-

nalist. She smiles
"A couple of months, into 1940, the headmaster was told, by one of our solid
boys, from a solid Christian family that, in the shower, he had caught an eye-

full of one of his friends, with a penis
That didn't look like... right, like his!"

"Jewish!" Then, the principal had another great idea:

"What about

those girls?" Somebody said:
"Rachel, Miriam, and Frieda, out of the shower put on their coats. I think I saw a Yellow Star,
Pinned on to their coats!"

The headmaster turned

them in. Madame told me what were her favorite read-

ings--
"Céline, Lucien Rabaté, Brasillach, George Montandon..."

And, she could have gone on, and on, especially checking out: the 1999, Publication

"L'antisémitisme de Plume, 1940-1944 "

(Pierre-André Taguiff, Paris: Berg International Editeurs, 1999)

"What a joy! That's us!"
(My book collection...)

She asked a local carpenter to build her extensive bookshelves, for her new Vichy collection.

(Her bookshelves were soon filled up, really quickly, having bought all those books, so quickly.)

Once, all those Jews in our school had disappeared, all students, who remained, sang Vichy Hymns, and, in the summer, went to work in the fields. They say that when Pétain visited all those fields, and,

When he found working youngsters in the fields, with

their shaven heads, he pat them (Later, they said, he'd chase after the female

staff, in his Vichy hotel.)
"Monsieur, L'Américian novelist:
That gives you a hint of what happened during the war, and how

happy all of us, solid Christians, were, right after the

                                    war!" "All?"

"Well, there's so much more, or so little to

                         remember, "Ain't

                         dat de Druf?"
          "Monsieur le Maire, could you introduce me to another
          family?"

His answer:

"No such time as you allude to will ever come…"

Jane Austin, "The Complete Novels" (NY: Random House, n.d.)

                         p.633 "They're all the same!"
"The men: medals!'
"The women, things they could pin onto their raincoats!"

"For my last question, at least for the moment, can you tell me what ever
happened to her husband?"

"He fell off…

                    A Jewish crane, in the harbor!"

I remembered, and I could see it in my eyes, A.O. Scott's review of the film:
"WILD," when he wrote:…
                         "Plot is the enemy of Truth…"

                         "I go
                         on
                         and
                         on

                         Go
                         on
                         and
                         on"

"The Essential Haiku, versions of Basho, Buson" edited by Robert Hass (NY:
Harper-Collins, 1994). p: 111 and 135

LAUNDRY

Left over Poetry

Pohème   The moon gloats

Sharks in blood
Frères Lumière

Gone in death
A third stands
Slays, the océan

.....

........Then, a signature, barely readable!

"DATZ REAL Poetry!"

(Now, that's an invaluable Truth!)

"Allez! Vous l'avez bien mérité »

Antoine Artaud : «Oeuvres complètes» tome IV (Paris: Gallimard, 1964) p.254

«You follow them with your eyes, you call to them... »

Robert Darnton, "Mesmerism, at the end of the Enlightenment in France" (NY: Schocken Books,1968)p. 2O.

Shabby Poet (lique hall pohetes)

More ARTTO! (For you, Artaud)

"Do I know nature, yet? Do I know myself—I mean, am I not nearly always fooling myself?"

Arthur Rimbaud, "A Season in Hell," "The Drunken Boat," Translated by Louise Varèse (NY: A New Directions, 1961)

"What Remains, and other Poems" (Serge Gavronsky, no publisher, yet...) "Awake and read!

"With my voice

It has awakened me"

The Poet Identifies himself

"I wanted to be a hand-glider, in the Olympics, above Grenoble, not far from
Courchevel." MORE

On the corner

of Lerven. And

Yev,

That's it!

No more of anything, written

for publication. No more Paris intellectuals. Should
All

First words

Of
any
em

Begin with a capital?

Huge popular crowds, near The Lion de Belfort.

Drinking black coffee, at the Café Daguerre.
Sit anywhere: Read

What's so   hot?

There?
A Statue of Liberty

La Goute D'OR

Street!   (For Moslems, with

prayer rugs) Napoleon brought down by Courbet

who,

In jail, painted flower portraits.
Mornings

Shit carriers in Seoul for...

SALE

Mid-yr sales, at the Bon Marché, measuring all that stuff in an overly-warm
store, on the 3rd
Floor.

(For more, check out my old future publication.

A REPETITION in a silence...)
Another voice, on stage...

Roland Barthes, "Elements of Semiology," Translated by Annette Lavers and
Colin Smith (NY: Hill and Wang, 1967) p.235

"In those oppositions, whose relation would in logic be a declaration of
exteriority, the two
Terms are equivalent."

TRUTH

(in a title) Is much better than

.....PLOT

Dorothea Tanning, "Between Lives: An artist and her world." (NY: W.W.
Norton and Company, 2001)p. 235

I'M MOVING RIGHT ALONG,

Trying

To get my story straight, that is, reducing plot, in order to play with other People's

Fake Truths!

If you can read me, you'll see how I distribute TRUTH, meaning SILENCE, in
order to avoid PLOT.

Truthpro-
sahic

"Monsieur, le maire, I really want to thank you for all your

help." I suspect
"I don't have to ask you, to yet introduce me to another family!

With your help, with that Family, I can make up what all the others

would say!"

(.....That's what a novelist is expected to do, that is, invent...)
testimonies!"

(And, thanks for that
Gauloise.)

(What a script that would

make!) "HOWEVER,

I didn't want to thank

him, also, For that cigar he had given me!

Stinks up my room! In

the meantime, I'll entertain myself, playing on my blue guitar.

"Like a man bent
over his guitar"

Wallace Stevens, "The man with a blue guitar" (NY:
Alfred A. Knopf, 1945) p.3

Loud, clanging church
bells

"Where they all gone? Those Jewish kids, gone?"

I see black-dressed women going in.

The priest semonizes.
You can hear a dormant silence.

(Did they know that Bormann was Hitler's aid? Had they
heard about Dresden and bombings?)

Women weep.   They do it

                                         Ev-
                                         ery
                                         Sun-
                                         day.

They walk to the RR station.

Leave wilted rose bouquets,
                              Left by the swinging doors.

On the tracks, to the left, they see an imaginary train, stationed on platform A.

When it rains

Older women go home.
                              Flip through memory albums.

They notice those Jewish children, wearing the school's blue uniform.

Sometimes, a mistake might have been made.
"Why didn't Madame Rigolo not tell them not to swim out, so far, during their
summer vacation?"

I remembered his birthday.

A photo shows him blowing out 13 candles.

(It must have been, around 4 o'clock, that Thursday)

                              "I speak with some hesi-
                              tation..."

John Williams, "Augustus" (NY: The Review of Books,

                 1971) p37

"They thought they were going on a trip!"
                 At that time, nobody knew where they were
                 going!

As for me, I went to Paris, on the rue de Sèvres, with my Leica, to catch winter sales.

Then, I decided to find number 93, rue de Lauriston, in the XVI arrondissement.

A beautiful garden, in the back, and, at street level, fake Greek statues, all men,
Nearly Naked: some bending, others, holding shafts of arrows and, in the front,
another group, But, this time, Roman copies of Greek ladies, all young ones.

I wondered, from what I knew, if, in their cellar, they had tortured members of
the Resistance?

And then, down the street, encrusted in the sidewalk, golden triangles, with
names on them.

(I was really, really thirsty,

But | knew those golden triangles meant Jews.)

I could smell good coffee, at the far corner of Lauriston.
                                                    Now, more yellow triangles...

                    Now, once again, I saw an elderly woman,

weeping. Kleenexs,
Weeping.
\
Crumbled on the sidewalk.

                    A bunch of wilted flowers, by the fence

"I COULD IMAGINE A GRAND-Père trying to recollect shatters of his

memory.

Then he added:

"Kids will be

Kids!"

His wife added a bouquet, by the

closed door. She slid her 2 euros in the

church box.
                    She followed her husband to the nearest métro stop.

She

loved Paris! All those stores!
                    All those well-kept parks!

                                        The smell of warmed-over marrons

            "Seuls les Français avaient le droit de parler librement. »

Man Ray : « Autoportrait » traduit de l'américain par Anne Guérin (Saint-Amand-
Montrond : Actes Sud, 1998) p.346

(She'd never, really, admit to her husband, how, every time they went to Paris
(dreaming like

                        "Mme Emma Bovary) now rarer and
Rarer.
                    They'd amble down, outdoor markets, like the one on Bld
Raspail.

Secretly, she dreamt of eating cornichons, and, in the Luxembourg garden,
"marrons glacés"

                        The coffee
                        was great!

She wasn't the only one who loved putting a second piece of sugar drown in
                                        her
coffee.

(The mind, at times, goes backwards...)
A well-dressed conductor (you've read about him...)

"You can tell who he is by his perfectly ironed, blue uniform, his white

                        HAND-
                        KER-
                        CHIEF"

Manuel Puig, HEARTBRECK SERIAL TANGO, translated by Jill Levine (NY: Vintage
Books, 1982) p.145.

                        He leaned
                        on the bar

And wept, in his official handkerchief.

Lots of noises and snot.

He's just read that the French government would meet the request of Nazis and Vichy, France, when they wrote:

> "Round them all up, all those Paris Jews, and bus them to the
>
> > Vel'd'hiv." (…Before becoming yet Another Holocaust Sta-
>
> > tistic.)

You've all read about them!

Trains took them to Drancy and, from there, to death.

> > "Then drive me from my com-
> > munity"

Mary B. Shelley: "Frankenstein" (NY:Classic Comics, Gilbenton Company, 1945)

n.p C'est lā le vrai	Right there true
Patriotisme	Patriotism
Il se transmet de…	Transmited from
Génération ā tra-	Generations tow-
Vers les millénaires	ward thousands of years

Intact

 ure   Pure

(sans mariage)

                 Your baguettes

          Francheezes   Without getting married

You   Married femmes
Intact

                    (Make me a martini, no movie clichés...)   To women

Dans un...   In

        «boiled meats, whole-wheat bread, small portions of dry vegetable... »

Michel Foucault: "The Use of Pleasure," vol.2, translated by Robert Hurley (NY: Vintage Books, 1986) p.112

Mauvais aire   Aweful

Raciale   Racial blood

...qui viennent altérer le   Coming

Sang de la   VOMIT   To change the

Race   Blood
                        Of the race

Doctor Martial

                        He played with his twins, in his
                        backyard

(He wondered if they had been drafts of a forgotten series of orders? Of forgotten Memories?)

"Please,
Shut the windows.   Too much of a draft

Or, could it have been, in agreement with his father's WWI insistence, to help out "True" France?

                        (Hain't dat always di

excuse?)

He whispered, to himself:
                        "Could my memory, please, echo
                        my memory?"
To fill in the gaps, he recited the beginning of a poem he had learned, in his

second lycée classe...

"The Inspector General had thick black hair, growing out of his ear- lobs."
Could he have been taken
for him?

Next morning, shaving, he saw, growing out of his nose, tufts of black hair.

"Where did you take them?"

Had he caught a cold, with all those win-

dows open?

On sunny days, conducting, he had that certitude of

going straight to:
Dachau

Or was

It

Auschwitz

(Spelling was never his strength.)
His third year teacher

gave him an 8 out of 20, as

a grade) "Here, in this coffin lies a dead man..."
Bertolt Brecht, "Selected Poems" translated by H.R. Hayes (NY: Evergreen
Original, 1959) p.127

(Around four, every morning, he feared he might be brought to justice for his
work...)

(With a little forehead, he might have read, in the NY Times, Tuesday,
December 16, 2014, Where René Bousquet, in 1942, had written:

"You should not hesitate to destroy any resistance you may encounter, among
these Populations."
And, he added:
"Transfer thousands of Jews to deportation camps."

(Somebody, in the bar, had already read all of that info. the day before.)

(Somebody said: "It's all on the phone!")

"Sometimes, I'm not at home, but I hear bulldogs growling, held on leather leashes"

My wife often picks up the phone.

A Heavy foreign   accent.

"The trouble with this
account..."

Michael Fried: "Absorption and Theatricality: Painting and the Beholder in the

Age of Diderot" (Berkeley: U of C Press, 1980) p.72
She shakes me out of a well-earned sleep.

Did she hear me snore, or, say something, when the sun hadn't yet come

out?

She says:

"Stop waking
me up!"

I say, looking at her, half hidden on her side of the bed:

"It's the same old story, of love (mine and yours!!) and

glory!"

I can still hear a guard yelling:

"To the barber..."
Next morning, I bought a copy of Le JOURNAL DU DIMANCHE. A captain is
quoted AS SAYING: "All The Enemies of the people should have their heads cut
off, or put on rafts, and have Them drown."

I never told my former teacher about

my job. But they did see my wallet

growing.
Protestant mothers

Wept

Catholic mothers

Wept

(Why not atheist mothers?)

(Jewish families, if they were lucky enough to get a piece of paper from a Vichy

subaltern, for a A price, could get out of Occupied France)

So many went to Marseilles.)

A US State Dept. official (Vartian Frey) had given visas to …(later, we knew, they were all Jewish men artists and
Women, like that Venitian Jew, Peggy Guggenheim.)

Then, we all went back to Mme. Rigolo's home.
                                    She served us, on a silver heirloom tray, the
traditional salami, ham, and cheese sandwiches, on slices of baguettes, with
bubbly white wine, served in her family glasses.

I could even say, that was a Sunday tradition.

                        "I'll walk with you past the Dragon movie house."

                        "I can't! It's all so….   dirty."

                    "Got to wash all those

dishes!"

                        The priest did some.
TIM PASSES.

                            (Don't it always?)

They whispered, to themselves:
                    "When that US novelist finally gets out of here, we'll celebrate!"

All of us, once again, went back to Mme. Rigolo, for her traditional Sunday
sandwiches.

                        "Wash him from our memories!"
By the way, someone asked, how did anyone ever find out our street
addresssses?
                            I received

A package, with a baby doll, a baseball bat, and, for me, silk

stockings! (How the devil, did someone ever find out my

street?)
In our local bar

LA VIE EN ROSE

After mass,
As we always do on Sundays, we walk to the cemetery.
                    Our future, reserved places!

Years later

Years after the end of the war, when the bar owner took down Pétain's por-

trait, Somebody sang

LA

VIE EN ROSE A chorus :

« La La La… ! »
In our memories, we had already died.

Still, on Sundays, there was always a voice, somewhere, back there, asking,
ritually:

                                        "Where did all our kids go?"

(During the Third Republic, there were 3000 Jewish officers and, 5 Generals, all

Jewish!) (And, lots and lots of Jewish teachers.)
On Sundays, you could always have someone remember how a city in the US
had founded a duplicate city, probably a Protestant one, which had opened for
high school Rejects.

An old man, his teeth jiggling, says:

                                        "Don't nobody ask me questions."

"Grand-père, tell me, once more, what happened to all those kids, their names,
Slowly Disappearing, on that plaque, on the wall of our RR station?"

His teeth jiggled.

He answered: "Never ask me about the past!"

She thought to herself:

"Why?" Later, somebody answered her question, and said:

FACTS

FACTS

FACTS

(He'd just read Dickens' HARD

TIMES.) Mme Cheval broke in.

Around August 16[th,] a German officer came to our town, looking for Jews.

I told him:

"A good Jew is hard to find!"

Veit Valentin, "The German People" (NY: Alfred K. Knopf, 1951)p. 567

She said: "Believe me, he spoke in such an elegant French! Believe me, I almost thought I might, one day, invite him for a glass of Calvados!"

He was so thoughtful!
"I can easily remember him paying for our picnic, on Sunday mornings, after mass!"

She said: "I'll never forget it, but in October, he paid for a round of beer, for all of us, at our favorite bar! You know, the one opposite City Hall and, across the street from our church!"

Another, good Christian,

said she remembered how he took our Blond to our dance, at our annual Lycée fête! Then, one day, I think it must have been our allies, the ones, you know, stationed in England, when half of our country was bombed out!

"Tell our novelist, what happened next."

"Well, on a midnight, in late July, we found him, dead and naked, with only a swastika on his belly, and a note:

"We'll kill
you all!"

The note was

signed:

Maquis"

The novelist: "Do you know what happened to that

body?" A whisper.

"They say, his body floated to the surface, once again, and docked, not

far from here!"

"Then what?"

"I'll tell you, but it's a weird story!"

"Go ahead..."

"Well, one day, Marie-Antoinette was delivered a letter, asking her to come,
as soon as possible, to see our facteur, you know, our mailman!"

She did.

She opened his front door.

She saw our conductor hanging from a rafter, and a note pinned to his sock.

"Chère madame,

Please tell all my elderly women friends, in town, how sad I am to

leave them, this way!"

Then, he added a more personal note:

"Please look under my bed."

I did.
I saw a pair of babouch- his slippers from...well... some North African country!
Then, under that same bed, a Hebrew Bible, and, you'll never guess what..."

"What?"

"A gold star! I kid you

non!" "He cried, when

he wrote that."

Then, he said, and you could tell by the water marks on the letter, how he had suffered, all those years, how he hated himself for wearing a French Catholic conductor's blue uniform, and, kill all our children! But he said he had to send his monthly check, back to his family. He said they had to get food."

"Anything else?"

"Well, he gave us very precise information as to his burial. He said that, under his bed, I'd find a red carry-on.
Inside, I'd find two red balls."

"He wrote that, when he was buried, the balls had to be inside that red carry-on, and...well, you'll never believe this, but he said, I should place those two red balls on his...well, he said it in English:
"His Red Balls, Express!"

I said to myself, because of those slippers, he must have been a Berber Jew!

On an autumn rainy day, all of us (really, I hadn't told anyone about the red-carry-on) walked behind his coffin.

It started raining, so all of us unfolded our old black umbrellas, and continued on our procession, behind his casket.

He was lowered into the earth.

Earth thrown on his wooden box.

I dreamt I threw my two red balls on

his lower parts....

Then, I really

knew what I had to do!
"Hello, could I speak to Marie-Antoinette?"

"This is "Josephine's Retirement Community."

"All our ladies have white table cloth! Marie-Antoinette is having her weakly check-up! I'll tell her you called! And,
You can try tomorrow. Best in the afternoon!"
The following afternoon, I did.

The phone operator said: "Bonjour!" (On my last call, she had said, in a very weary tone of voice:
"Au revoir!"

I went home.

The next day, I called again, and got to talk to Marie-Antoinette.

I gave her, with newsreel precision, about all that had happened! She couldn't believe her ears, and, she said, in a muffled voice:

"Alas, poor conductor, I knew him well…"

She cried.

An attendant's voice broke in.

"Time for our morning sleep!"

She said, in a kind voice. Time

remained the same.

"I speak with some hesitation…"

John William, "Augustus" (NY: The Review of Books, 1971) p. 37

The lycée philosophy teacher, said to me, "as an American novelist:
"Would you please give meaning to a voice?"

I answered: "I've got some M&M in my pocket, just for you!"

She said: "I hate US candies!"
My mother said, when US troops arrived in our town, they poisoned us, with their candies and… silk stockings, for all our young girls. I was one of them, I hate chuckles."

Broom words

Somebody, seeing the officer's soaked

body, An older man, said:

"put something on him!"

At that very moment, he took a picture of his naked body and, later, pinned it to his wall, above his bed.

As our village slowly recovered, both the body and our calm, the priest reminded all of us, that we shouldn't miss our film club,

"Today." he reminded us, the subject was " M.Monroe, walking over grated cheese," and her...her skirt flying up! Got that?"

"He added: "for our next meeting: We'll take up American pilots, during WWII."

Somebody said, he would order two poached eggs, on buttered whole wheat toast, a small orange juice, and a cup of Greek coffee.

The lycée teach. had insisted, we'll go over to our new American arrival, and what we could do for him, if he continued asking questions of all of us! And, he made it clear, he knew what was our place, during the war."

"Meaning?"

"Not that again!......."

He came back with his 1938 camera, probable bought at a fair in Warsaw, after the war. He took at least ten pictures.

"To one who took pleasure..."
"The Life and Opinions of Tristam Shandy" (NY: Bonie Liveright, MCMXXX)p.359
Somebody else said:

"Read:"

The

RAYMAYA Somebody added:

"Pascal's

Thoughts" Somebody else, barged in:
"The Little Red Book"

Somebody else, added:

"HA HA HA!"

I guess we all knew philosophers cheated, when they convinced us that we should
                        Take: footnotes, very seriously.

TITLE

                            FOOTNOTES

"Watch time evolve. Add to that, a personal comment!"

All of us made believe we pushed our way into a local

WINE cave!

Women wept.
Then, our weekly procession to the plaque on the RR wall, with all the children's names.

An aunt cried out:

        "I told them to be extra-careful, if they decided to dive off that rock!"

        Another mother said:

                "I told him not to get toO close, to the depth of the river!"
That was 21 years ago.

At home, they lit three candles.

"Where have they all gone?"
In fact, nobody got their kids, back.

(A parent said: "that, at least, 3 male bodies, spread out on that rock, had wound up in an
American painting!
Probably a Thomas Eakins.?)

One was in the water.

(Did he ever paint good-looking boys in the water?")

"Where have they all gone?"
Our priest went to the Bon Marché, on rue de Sèvres, to buy white shirts he could wear, on his day off.

REPETITION

The American novelist decided to go to 93, rue de Lauriston, in the 16th arrondissement.
Beautiful gardens, so well kept up by Spanish day-laborers.

He remembered having read, in a post-WWII, paper, that Resistance fighters, known as the "Maquis," were tortured, there, in that cellar, now, covered over by plastic flowers.

I was in a hurry, but I did read a plaque, saying how many Jews, there, had been tortured to death.

How that Pétain crowd would have been delighted to plant copper plates, on certain sidewalks, as a sign of a good conscience! Do what they had to do, for instance, in Berlin, with little gold triangles, with names of Jews, in round-ups in Jewish neighborhoods, trucked off to their deaths.

"But what indeed, can a civilization be worth, which at all time of dire need…"

Leon Trotsky, "On Literature and Art" (NY: A Merit Book, Pathfinder Press, 1979) p. 170

Once again, I could smell that great Turkish coffee, or was it Greek? I sat there, ordered coffee.

In that place, newspapers, held by long wooden sticks, held the Figaro and Le Monde.

Now,

once again, She took out a Kleenex.
She whispered to herself:

"I shouldn't be worried! He'll be back, very soon."

A baby-seater said, in mangled French:
"Kids will be kids! As one of them fell off a swing, and bruised his knee!

An adult you knew, a conductor on his day off, wearing a

well-ironed Shirt, undershirt, and underwear…"

Manuel Puig, "Heartbreak serial Tango" (NY" Vintage Books: translated by Jill Levine, 1982) p.145

He leaned on the copper bar, left foot, on the

well-ironed bar.

He had read that the

French gov. would agree with the request of Nazis and Vichy, to round-up all Jews, initially rounded up, and then sent to Drancy, waiting for a train to take them to their deaths, taken there, by the SNCF, the French RR.

"Then drive me from my community"

Mary B. Shelly, "Frankenstein" (NY: Classic Comics, Gilbenton Company, 1945) n p.

(A novelist does not, necessarily, remember every place he's ever visited, all the people he had interviewed, and yet, he could never forget that town…)

"Here, in this zinc coffin

Lies a dead man…"

Bertold Brecht, "Selected Poems" translated by H.R. Hayes (NY: Evergreen Original, 1959) p.127.

With a little forehead, he might have read, in the NY Times, Tuesday, December 16, 2014, where René Bousquet, in 1942, had written:
"You should not hesitate to destroy any resistance you may encounter among these populations, transfer thousands of Jews to deportation camps."

Somebody, in the bar, had read all that information, the day before.

(Someone said: "It's all on the phone.")

"Sometimes, when I'm not home, I hear bulldogs growling, on their leather leashes, all

night
long!"

Sometimes, when I'm not home, my wife picks up the

phone. She says to me:

           "I think he spoke with a heavy

foreign accent!"

           She shakes me out of my well-earned

sleep.
"Honey, call this number back! That's what he asked, in that strong foreign accent."

Benedict de Spinoza: "Ethics and on the Improvement of the Understanding" (NY: Barnes&Noble Books, 2005) p.205

I said to her: "do not talk to me when I'm trying to sleep, after a rough day's work! Besides, I know who's calling, with that heavy German accent!"

           "It's always the same old
           story!"

In the back of my memory, I can still hear that American novelist, asking, all of us, highly disturbing questions!

Next morning, drinking my coffee (a bit under-heated!) I skim over the Journal DU DIMANCHE, where a captain is quoted, as saying: "All the enemies of the people should be in prison or killed. Let me remind you (he continued) that, during the French Revolution, all enemies of the Revolution were herded on a raft, not far from here, and, all were drowned. No trains needed! No sleeping bunks needed, no food prepared.
        Why don't we take a page, out of that practice!"

I never uttered a word about what I was doing...

Nearly everybody saw how much I had, in my over-sized pocket, once a month.

           Protestant mothers wept

           Catholic mothers wept

Then, all of us, as I tell my American novelist, we all went back to Madame Joie.

She served us, on her heirloom tray-- tiny salami sandwiches, on crispy baguettes, and small pastries, with mounds of cream, on top.

("When that American slips away, we'll forgive his insistent, questions!")

(“I'll walk with you, as far as the

Dragon.”)
The priest offered to wash the silver tray.

Madame Joie said, she'd do the rest, in the kitchen.

Edouard Drumont, «La France juive » (Paris: Ernest Flammarion. 1986) p. 205

Somebody told us how many Jews hadtaught our children, in our universities,

in our lycées.

“Grand-Père, tell us what it was like!”
Now, we HEARD what he remem-

bered. “Whether it is reality or not, I

don't know.”
“Poems of Fernando Pessoa” (NY: The Ecco Press, 1986) p. 108

“I was confused with the problem…”

“C.G. Jung: “Memories, Dreams, Reflections” (NY: Vantage Books, 1968)

p.116

“All the kids, right here!” He said.
His teeth jiggled.

“Please, don't remind me of my

Past-present!

I
,

My memory's flagging!”

I whispered to myself:
“How I wished to forget!”

Looked like his memory had been cleaned out of all his mind's

notebook!

All I wanted were:

FACTS-

FACTSFACTS (Dickens' "Hard Times")

But, a few years later, I was studying European history in a NY State

college.

They asked me the same, repetitive question:
"You grew up in France, during the war. Tell us what it was like!"

"In my second year, I took a course in creative History writing.
I tried to invent everything I
hadn't lived through!"

"I invented a good guy, accused of a horrible crime."

He invented what he was supposed to
say.

Twelve make-believe
jurors

Lis-
tened,
intently

"Who was your instructor?"

"An American novelist!"

I sent my first (over-worked) short story and...you'll
never believe this, but that story started me on my new profession!"

(Even the jury applauded! They convicted him of dallying with young boys in
his neighborhood!)

He was sent to a mental institution, up-state, for five years of rehabilitation, if
he promised never to do that, again!

Parents, in the audience
All applauded, especially parents of young boys.

Outside, the police told them to report any young adult who looked like a
prospective tickler of young boys.

"Promise, get your eyes together, and report anything that looks suspicious!"

The jury reached its verdict.
The judge agreed.

Slavoj Zizek: "The invisible Remainder, on Schelling and Related Matters" (London-NY: Verso. 1996) p. 146

The judge was quite clear:

> "Three years rehabil-
>
> itation!" Parents
>
> applauded.

"In the empty courtroom..."

Franz Kafka, "Trial" (NY: Schocken Books. 1970) p.49

His attorney had made a half-hearted attempt, saying his young client was mentally disturbed. On the witness stand, when he swore, and he swore again, and again, he said he was totally innocent.
> "The advance fixing of a termi-
> nation..."

Jacques Lacan,"translated by Anthony Wilden (NY: A Delta Book, 1975) p. 75

Nobody believed him:

> "Here's proof:
>
> I'm only 22, and I live in a violin neighborhood."

> The judge straightened out his robe.

Then, he added, as if that might have changed the verdict:

> "As of the age of 12, I played a Suzuki violin, as a solo violinist."

"My teacher, Louis de Clerval, a recent émigré from the South of un-occupied France, from a long line of aristocratic family of PROTESTANTS, destroyed during Montaigne's century."

He added: "As soon as I got to the US, I fell in love with young violinists."

"He

reiter-

ated:

But parents, in the audience, yelled out:

      "He's a pervert! We knew that, a few weeks later!"

The judge added to that sentence, a more precise punishment:

"He's a sicko"
And, he added: "He shall be sent to an upstate mental institution."

And, he added: "There, he'll be treated for sexual hallucinations, as a sex offender, all because he put his arm around a 12 year old's shoulder, as he was misreading his violin concerto.

The local police called the parents of the 12 year old, failed violinist, and grabbed that Protestant, odd-ball teacher.

"When he gets out, if you see him, in the neighborhood, do not hesitate, call

     us!"

     The local paper made him a headline offender
"The trouble about the good man, is that he's only one hundredth part of a man: posed a serious problem is that he's only one part of a man."

D.H. Lawrence, "Selected Literary Criticism" (NY: The Viking Press, 1956) p.257

After their applause, parents left the

courtroom. A mother was overheard

saying:

     "He posed a real problem!"

"He looked at us, during the trial, as if he was thinking, when our boy grows up,

he'd be there." Check out Dylan Thomas, "Portrait of the Artist as a young dog"

(Liverpool: C. Tinling, 1940) p.86
His medically-trained psychologist-lawyer succeeded in having his sentence commuted.
EHCO ECHO

Ech (o)

In the background, violins played Bach. Someone hummed the Marseillaise.

"Narcissus, in Ovid's"liberTertius" (Metamorphosis and Héroides)

Michel Foucault, "Language Counter –Memory, Practice." Ed. with an
Introduction by Donald F. Bouchard (NY: Ithaca, 1997) p.165

Post-
WarNEW
INFORMA-
TION

The Social Studies teacher, only 23 years old, had ogled 14 year old girls, while
his left hand played with a hard rubber ball.

A quick trial, immediately following Violin's.

Sentenced, the violin and the Social Studies teacher, together, but this time,
in a prison upstate.

15-20 years

Both knew they hadn't done right.

"None the less, the two expositions are compatible

enough..." Edmund Husserl, "Ideas" (London: Collier

Books, 1975) p.145

A short
time later

Old police files

"The truth? Who has provided the truth?"

Milan Kundera: "Farewell Waltz" translated by Aron Asher. (NY: Harper
Perennial, 1971) p.122

"This is your captain Bice. Do you hear me?"
    "Yes, sir!"

"Ok! Drive as fast as you can, to 690 Marquis Bld."

"Yes, sir!"

"Be right there!"

They parked I their police car, in front of the two-car garage, under-

neath the basketball hoop.

They ask:

"Where's his room?"

"Upstairs, to the left."

"Captain, we're almost

there!"
They opened his door and, right in front of them, a vertical series of 7 built
shelves, with five books on each shelf.

"Hey! Take a look at his

culture!" Jane Austin

St. Au-

gustine

Thomas

Bern-

hard

Brecht
Bellow

d...

below: Foster Freud Honeyday Goethe

Giraudoux

d...

below: Nöel
Nin

Nabokov

Nizan

Orwell

                                d...
                                urr,
                                e:e
                                nd-
                                hal
                                nd-
                                ho-
                                ro
                                hef

....

("Hope

we got all the spellings right!")

      "Exciting" "Yes"

"Provocative"

                  Fresh and liberating:
                        "We purposely left out: Under "M":

"Le marquis de Sade: "Three Complete Novels: "Justine, Philosophy in the Bedroom and Eugénie de Franval."

(NY: Evergreen Black Cat Book, translated by Richard Seaver, and Austin

Wainhouse, 1965) . "Under his pillow, to the left:

                  "Kama Sutra" p. 128 and a copy of
                  Molinier's photographs, opened to page 28

                For his
birthday

His parents,

Having been seduced by an Iranian film, decided to rename their son:

Massroom Bangla.

                              Father lit an e-cigarette

                              Mother did the same

And, as a result, before being convicted, at the age of 3, for perversion with little girls, Massroom cried out:

> 'est
> la
> ie!"

When I got out of reform school, I took up p. 51, and read through it once

more. Madeline Gins: "Word Rain" (NY: Grossman Publishers, 1969) n.p.
For his next birthday, he requested his parents give him:

> A Ralph Lauren dia-
> mond watch

The year before, he had requested a Sèvres porcelain vase, with lots of swans on it, made for the Paris World's AFFAIR, 1900.

In the middle of the night, just like his father, he got up to

piss. He broke his vase.
Then, he returned to his caliphate, as he had baptized his room.

He DID HAVE A DREAM, did have a Dream-- COMING OUT OF OUR FAMILY TOILET. There, he dreamt of an FB1 interview--

(Coming out of the piss room, he was interrogated by

the FBI.) He wrote it down on a yellow piece of paper.
(".." "................
....)"
(Little did he suspect that his brain had been impregnated by his father's sperm)

(Little did he suspect that.............)

"This opinion is doubtlessly not always expressed so FRANKLY..."

"French Utopias, An Anthology of Ideal Societies," Edited by Frank E. Manuel and Fritzie P. Manuel (NY: Schocken Books, 1971)p. 288

> He smirked

All quiet on the fiddle front.

The day after the trial, fiddle-carrying kids, all 12 yrs. Old, yelled

out: "Drop dead:

"He's a fagola!"
Then, she added: "If he ever came in your proximity, run as fast AS YOU can CALL,
BUT DO NOT DROP YOUR FIDDLES …"

"Kick em' out of our neighborhood!"

(A kid whispered,   "kick his testicles."
Nearby parents, swinging on their newly painted white veranda, whistled with
pleasure.
                   "You see how careful our kids really are…"

"Thus, the rabble of mankind look upon these.."

Frederic R. White "Famous Utopias of the Renaissance: Thomas Moore,
Campanella, Francis Bacon&others" (NY: Hendricks House, inc. 1955) p.73.
"How observant! Must be their basketball coach!"
A father remembered a childhood quote:

                    "All's well that's remembered

well!" "We've finally got rid of that queer!"
A prison warden, in an upstate meta-rehab., was heard sighing:
                   "Before he's freed, let's put him with Social Studies!"

A key

A lock

2 matresses

1 above the other

Thus, for a brief moment, Violin and Social Studies found themselves talking to
each other, reminiscing.

                                        "Yes, here

            we are!" "We are—"

        "Who?"

"Who's?"

who?"

A further question:
Tell me, or translate:

"We have already considered the many inhibitions and deffilcul-

ties..." Simone de Beauvoir, "The Second Sex" (NY: A Bantam Book,

1953)p. 146.

"YOU into ME"

"With you, too, you..."

Paul Celan," Snow part" translated by Ian Fairley (Riverdale-on-Hudson, 1960,
Sheep Meadow Press) p. 161

"Could I be half of a self?"

<u>"We are two segments of a world,</u>
<u>each one the other's double."</u>

(Brooklyn: "Long News in the Century" (1993) P.65.

A THROW AWA\\\\\\\\\\\\\\\\\\\\\\\\\\\\\\\\\\\\\

\\\\\\\\\\\\\\\\\

"A throw-away self?"

"Or, a terrible thought: an absence of a unitary self?"

(Out of the alphabet, a throw-

away self...) "We as

duplicates..."

"We are like conjoined Morandi

bottles"
"Didn't Mallarmé...?"

"Stop, with that series of quotes!"

"A piece of prose"

                              "Nothing more to write..."

"But, as a candid critic, I would ask you if the mirror can be considered..."

"George Meredith:
          "The Order of Richard Feverel" (NY: The Modern Library, 1927) p.277

As they prepare to leave their communal cell,

Once again, the guard says to himself:
          "They're convinced that I would find it difficult to replace them!"

André Gide, "The Immoralist" translated by Richard Howard (NY: Vintage Books,

1970) p.83 "Let's

                    flip a euro

"Let me/me sleep!"

                         Gloom filters
                         through.

Hovers over their "self's"

"We have already considered the many inhibitions and difficul-

ties..." Isaiah Berlin, "The Power of Ideas" (Princeton UP, 2000)

p. 223

                              One says to the other:

"We are a singular double!"
 And then a Dickenson quotes:
                         "Alone, I cannot be" (298)

                    "We Two looked so

alike..."

(1862)

"I'm Nobody! Who are

you?" (288)

And again: "Love—

though art high

I cannot climb thee…" (453)

Proof:

"You see what I see!" A spawned self.
"Men dream of what they do during the
daytimes."

Sigmund Freud, "The Interpretation of Dreams," translated by James Strachey
(NY: Basic Books, 1965) p.73

A guard unlocks the cell door.

"As I am You, we're an "/EYE"/Me/…A dydactic couple in

A mir-

ror of words. "They knew each other so well to pretend

anything."
D.H. Lawrence, "Sons and Lovers" (NY: Viking Press 1973) p.282

ME "Me two
Me, too, I speak me!

"So, too…"

"Blinded by …
a "ME/I"

"All Hands"   "One on a

    folding deck" "I'm"

    'I'm"

Max Frisch, "Homo Faber" (NY: Abelard Schuman, 1959) p.79

"We had no sooner shaken hands, than he sat down on the edge of my (bunk)"

A prison, like any other prison, whether here or here or a there, here...wherever that may be, on an island, for instance, or a city's "downtown."

"You first!"
"We closed our "me,"

                              Eye closed.

"We saw, on the wall, a Belgium tapestry."

"Two--were immortal twice.

"Emily Dickenson, see below, p. 200.

Then, once again, for the last time, one says to the other: says:

"You, re my mask!"   (I/Me
Strip

 Turn in my prison garb.

          Now, each other (the other) turns in his prison
uniform. Outside,

          You/You

  hears

                                        A TROLLEY pushing by.

Now, a violin's ball,   bounces off the edge of the hoop

          Now:

          "A round of fiddles playing Bach..." (Louis Zukofsky, "A"-1)

Always, the same old remembrance of a vio-

lin teacher. (His father was away three times a

month.)
  Always, the same old story.

"Alas!"

That's what he said, untying his tie, before putting on his pyja-

mas. As per usual, mother kissed him on both cheeks.
She knew,

In the meantime, kids were cycling on their birthday

gifts. One fell.
One fell on top of him.

       (Was that a future remembrance of a cycling
       desire?)

          From a front porch…

"If you do not cycle correctly, I'll call the police, right away, and they'll
confiscate all your…"

And he added: "I'll tell all your mothers…" (No violin mirroring.)

There she was, with a long knitting needle, on her front porch, sitting on her
rocking chair.

Daddy lifted his voice:

    "God damn it! The postman didn't throw my paper on the front porch."

          Kids stare at him.
Around noon, he bit into a mangled burger.

Mother cried out: "Stop with that burger shit! It's terrible for your

         health!"

"I told

       you, a thousand times"
"Fathers will be…"

He cushioned his contradictions, under his left-side pillow.

Dreamt of the Glanum, not far from centre ville, st. Rémy, and lots of other
Roman ruins.

After hearing a suspicion "next," I developed a frightening disbelief in my mind.

In his dream, he heard himself ask:

"Where have they all gone? (Probably haunted by the disappearance of all the boys, who had gone swimming, during the first week of their summer vacation."

On her side of the bed, she dreamt about two neighbors, who had become

one.

Then, an imagined phone call:
Saigyo: "Mirror for the moon"

> Translated by William LaFleur (NY: New Directions, 1977) p.9

Nobody could really imagine two in

one. "Where was one born? Where

was one born?"
(Schools? Diplomas?)   Marriage (if any) Jobs?

   Though, in one column, (on the back page of the NY Times Sport section, his picture on top. You could read where he had gotten his doctorate in Russian, his wife's family, where she had gone to college. What did her father do? Her mother?

THEN

Above his picture:

His colleagues deeply regret his passing.
His inspiration helped all of us get through the last Wall Street events.

For his integrity, his guidance ...(you fill in the rest...)

What was her position. His? How he had learned how to play the violin. And his best friend become a social studies teacher, in a private school, on the Upper East Side?

   One out of one said, said: "Who's going to write my obit? (I hope they'll find good of me(s) pictures!)"

>   "If I should die
>   Read only

This

                                              Of me"

           There

           I was!

           Not a SOUL in the dining room!

           Or
"O my brother! Do not leave me..."

  "The Poems of Longfellow" (NY: A Modern Library Book, nd)p.216

(I'm Basil Rathbone and Moriarty.)
                                    S h u s h   Both of us Are.

(At a fête, I/I was asked to make a wish. I said (after a considerable time had elapsed)

"I'm not Hitler"

                    "Cover your medals!"

                    "No one, probably, had ever believed that the will of a god
                    kept parallel lines..."

                    John Stuart Mill, "Auguste Comte and Positivism" (Ann Arbor

  Paperbacks, The University of Michigan Press, 1961) p. 47

(How much time remained for both of us, ONE/ONE?)

                              Poetry?

Were we blessed by unforeseen circumstances to act in our play? You/Prose/You...

  "Then, I heard:

  "Next!" (I so wanted to empty my

  bowels!)
                         "Any one left?"

A New Jersey American boy scout yelled out: "No,

Sir!"

He remembered himself, when he was a baby "self"
A policeman, sidling/ on his beach buggy, said:"...

He walked over, placed a used French flag over the kid's body, mine.

            "Get that kid dressed or else..."

I remember him,

He took a photograph, and said he loved to take pictures of little baby boys!
            Saying he loved to take pictures of little naked baby boys!

Then, he waved us on.

"Back to your bikes!" He said, smiling.

            "Don't climb up, on your uppity high horse!"
We waved him a long good-by.
He spotted us, once more, down the beach.

Once more,
And how could I ever forget that!
            He asked if he could take a better picture of our little, naked boy?
"Didn't have I ever told you, at the right beginning, what it was like to wear an
electronic bracelet around your ankle?"

"Me, too!"

                    Everything was up
                    to date, in New
                    York-Chicago City!

Who can really remember that, one day, for a marriage, a violinist was needed?

And again, somebody who really knew American history, by heart, just to set
that, even, in its right polemical place?

From afar, you could hear:

                    "O my brother, do not
                    leave me!"

"The Poems of Longfellow" (NY: A Modern Library Book, nd) p.216

Then, how could he ever forget his mirror image?

Both walked into a formal Hotel dining room, around Easter time.

                     Convention, the time of the annual MLA Convention Round Tables.
Flags on so many undergraduate colleges, beginning with inaugural letters like:
Bard College, Barnard... And an assortment of language/lit., supposedly, all
chairs of that dept.

All of them, seated, right there, with a small, plastic bottle of water, on rounded
tables, just in case...

After the interview, I congratulated the way she was dressed, and, if she wanted
to meet some of her future possible "others?"
I asked her,
           if she would like to join us, for a Chinese meal, on a Broadway,
           upstairs?

Then, my vacation.

I happily left the USA for France, to work on my translations and essays on
contemporary, French Women Poets.

I received a special delivery letter, telling me to go, immediately, to the Dean

Quickly as possible.
                     "I did."
"She accused you of blatant profiling when you applauded the beauty of her
Nigerian dress."

"She accused you, in that upstairs Chinese restaurant, when you asked her what
she wanted to drink.

The dean, then sadly continued.

"An insult!"
 "Didn't you know women, from her African country, don't drink?"

 "Didn't you know that, when you asked her if you could help her find an
apartment? You were barging into her private life?"

She's taking you

to court.

"We'll get you a top college lawyer's firm!"
                    They confiscated my computer.

They knew I taught Sade and, they knew that I had used the word:

                    "Libertinage."

            "Could you tell us what that means?"
                    (My Park Avenue firm.)
I Explained.

They looked at me, as if I were being cross-ex-

amined. "Thank you!"
I gave them all a c+, and thanked them for their curiosity, as if they were all
Freshmen.

A hearing.

The administration never told me the end result of that pre-trial.

I spotted
An 18th century model of researcher.

"You're speaking, this afternoon!

            What's your speech?"

A quick answer:

                    "Sade and gastron-

omy!"
He invited me to share an outdoor breakfast, on his veranda, out in Nevada,
with animals within an eye's range!"

I did.

He loaned me his rifle.

"Shoot, when they're in your sight!
                    Good luck!"

He opened his huge Frigidaire, and placed my four-legged victim, next to his.
"That should last me through next   X-mas!"

He asked me if I knew who was the guest

speaker. "Allen Ginsberg."

"Is that the Lower East Side,

queer?" Social Studies ap-

plauded.
He had read an anthology of Lower East Side poets reading at the Judson
Church, against the war in Vietnam.

The Chicago Police rushed to the speaker's podium. "You're

coming with us, to the station!"

"You can't be queer

"here!"

Social Studies teacher moaned:

"This isn't Hitler country!"

in a whisper: "I'll never spend more time in jail!"
A Russian professor was heard saying: "Ladies, cover your see-through bodies."

And then, somebody, he might have been a NY city...
A "Poet," He asked how much time he had to read and, even, and perhaps,
answer questions from some queer hater.

Some junior professor, recently tenured, and so...he thought he hadn't a fear
of administration condemnation: said:"
                    "Fuck that shit! Who needs to remember Katmanddoudo!"

"I said to him, during the coffee break: coffee and doughnuts, he'd better do
better work or I couldn't write him a decent letter of recommendation!"

Later, he was hired by an East Side private school, to replace the Social Studies
teacher, off on a Foundation grant.

He didn't know if that would help him get hired in a good college, like the one

in the city.

Actually, that Ph.d doctoral candidate, in contemporary Russian lit. and language, was a decent guy.

Later, in the school headmaster's office, an old teacher, about to resign herself to a retirement community party, said:

"How come they have them sing that patriotic anthem, without first reading all

about...

He too, had forgotten the author of the Marseillaise...

A Piecemeal prose

Silence, do you hear? On the corner of your fervor, and settle down your needs for after birth playfull would make his first move from comma to comma, henceforth, in an advanced hypothesis, generally accept the writer's death, without thinking of where his body's ashes shall rest, and this would make an adequate minor alternate with a feeling for the doubt

After the birth of somebody's twins, always looking right and left against a white background, generally acceptable, as of their first success. Later, much, later, at someone's discretion, accompanied by a sketch, on his screen, a bibliography, at the end of thought. She was auto-convinced that all things were only truths displaced.

"After all those letters of recommendations, wasn't it time to salvage my own being??"

A Spanish mother said: "They should all memorize our Spanish anthem! In any case, I'll take it up at the next parents' meetin!"

The principal agreed.

She feared that, if anything went wrong, her father would be shipped back to the old country, and she'd never see again.

She said, in her whisper:

"Do they actually believe that we're the scum of the earth?"

She whispered to her colleague:

"Sing us our national anthem!"

"One day, I'll get my revenge, and they'll all sing my national..."

A group of activists said, in a chorus, they would take a guided tour of China, and then, go back to their children and their teacher, and tell them all, how wonderful the schools were, especially in math, even though, all of them, had to come to school, every day, holding the little red book, and memorize the great leader's red speeches.

Yan-ze, an exchange student, from her"red" country, suggested we listen to her grand-mother's suggestion and appreciate new China in the making, via the grandmother's voice, via Yan-ze.

At another session, made a special point of mentioning a senior faculty, who made it quite clear that sodomy and pederasty were considered ultimate signs of a degenerate mind, especially in China!

Vernon A. Rosario: "The Erotic imagination, French Histories of Perversity" (NY" Oxford UP,1997) p.73

Her grand-father also insisted that the group had to fully appreciate 17th century paintings, with a selection from that century's Mustard Seed Garden's manual of painting.

Somebody repeated: "Familiarize yourselves with the

                                                T'ang

                                                Dynas-

                                                ty The

                                                Sung

                                                period

                                                The

                                                Ming

                                                Period

"And,listen to Rameau's nephew." (?)

"The students we met had all mesmorized passages from the Little Red Book. (We were forced to do so...) And... you must avoid gasping at all of our imitation sexual Indian cave drawings"

The principal had had an hour-long chat with the prospective Social Studies instructor. She whispered to herself:

"That guy really knows his stuff!"

On his CV, she read that he could also double as a Russian teacher.
That really did it:

Also, how would he deal with FDR's love affair, without ever suspecting that
Eleanor knew all about them, and that, all the time.

Stalin.
In the back of his mind, he thought he really had something to say about

Boys...
"Savage systems of classification are based on extremely precise observations."

Clande Lévy-Strauss and the "Making of Structural Anthropology, translated by
Mary Baker (Minnesota, The University of Minnesota Press, 1998)p 148
(In the meantime, ONE) had nearly falling in love with the well--dressed, red cap,
bell-hopper.

He gave it lots of thought.

"Tuesday, clean bed, no fleas for the first time"

Ezra Pound: "Canto" LXII (NY: New Directions, 1983), p. 374

In parenthesis, he would always have wanted to be hired in a Princeton High
School, not far from a horse farm, or anywhere else, within that world!

He counted his options!

He gave it lots of thought!
"Would there be a perfect meeting with a Wall Streeter?"

"Anything else?"

(He whispered.)

He swallowed.

(In fact, he could not stop his memory from stuttering with his

memory)

He approached an alphabet   Sat at an

university table. "Take a

seat."
In the meantime, they all rehearsed, in front of a giant mirror, before entering
the main Ball Room   for their interviews.

One prospective candidate asked if anyone knew where was the nearest toilette?
He quoted Apollinaire's 2 lines:
> "I'm fed up
> I'm going to piss"

He walked, ten paces, to the Men's room.
Stood, hummed, and pissed,
As others did the same, talking- all the while, about the time it had taken them
to reach that cold and windy, damn city!

You could hear zippers noising-upwards.

But his double sat next to him, as if both, as ONE, were considering being hired

by an institute, specializing in decoding secret documents, in Russian and French,

probably sent by two French- Soviet CA agents.
On their way back from the Interview ballroom, two men, wearing raincoats,
just like in a movie, showed their badges to the three guards, paid to keep
strangers out, at least those who didn't pin their id's. on their left lapels.

The interviews were of little, respective interest.

But, the pinned-up individuals, made a quick proposal:
> "Would you like to save
>
> America?"   ("Save
>
> it from Soviet spies?")
"You have been chosen! You will be sent to D.C, directly to CIA HQ, secretly,
located beneath Arlington Cemetery."

The chair of the French department, asked one, if I/I could comment on Fourier's
theory of love.

I/I answered.

As it turned out, those two wore British raincoats, and yet, both looked like CIA agents, or two Morandi bottles.

Both were told to pack up their belongings, and put them in a red-carry-on.

"in the meantime, both of one..."

"Do not forget your bathing suits and...your electric toothbrush!"

After a brief intro, the two informed their hirers of their identity. Their interviewers knew all about that!

(They whispered)   "Why were we picked?"

Real ques-

tion: Between ages of   age :

"29 to 30 yrs old."

"You'll be paid a monthly salary, plus expenses"

(The two CIAS wore Burberrys.)

"How much each month?"

"Cannot divulge that, at this moment!"

One/One was told HE would be immediately sent to Biarritz, and put up at the Napoléon- Cavour Hotel.

"If you're so inclined, check out the bathing suits-drop-
pings area, downstairs, out of your window!"

"AS OF YOUR ARRIVAL, French, and other journalists, will try to betray your innocence, with a barrage of questions."

"Do not reveal your name..."

"But, you will quickly be asked:

"can you tell a Soviet from an Albanian?"

"In the meantime, both of us..."

Marinetti, "Selected Writings." Edited and with an Introduction by R.W. Flint, and translated by R.W Flint and Arthur A. Cappotelli (NY: Farrar, Strauss and Giroux, 1972) p.43

"Only the best..."
                    "You're it!"

            One whispered to the other:
"Grab your future!"
  "Besides, apart from getting an elegant monthly

salary..." "How much?"

(they rerpeated.)
"Much!"

"Besides, both of you have been chosen for two highly secret mis-

                        sions." The other one says:

"Your mission is..."
                    "Redon's Silence?"

The other one whispered: Goya's

                "Grande promesse

Contre des morts"
  CIA continued:

"There's a beautiful young lady, in Toulouse, who sends secret information to
the Soviet Union on the latest scientific progress on the design of the new
Mystère airplane!"

So...You, as a French language specialist you, have been chosen to follow her
every telephone call, her E-M...
                Got that? Her every movement..."

        In unison, both mouthed a line from Anne Lauterbach:

"And the light reached all the way into the dark..."

        "If in Time, Selected Poems, 1975-1997" (NY: Penguin, 1997) p.109

        Then, another, a musical voice, near breakfast time, rang HIS/HIS
        doorbell:

"Your Breakfast!"

85

The manager had already whispered to US/I I : that sweet, friendly potatoes, would accompany our scrambled eggs.

"So, you are our French specialist!
You have been chosen to follow that French spy, and check out exactly what she's sending to the Soviet Union!"

(In the meantime, that is, waiting for thosefriendly fries, ONE/ONE say the two to themselves) "stop mouthing…"

Both-self really wanted to go to the Dragon Movie House, see a show, any show, to pass the morning time away.

They walked, hand in hand.

On the Marquee:

"The Pleasures of Pain"

Richard Abel: The Ciné goes to town, French Cinema-1896-1914, Updated and expanded version. (Berkeley: University of California Press, 1998) p.117

"How about, just Looking at an Erotic Film in the

"Eye"?" Then, with four eyes closed:

"Fun,

ain't it?" "In any, case, words like that, are now out-of-

date!"
Now, both ONES wondered, if it wasn't time to recite,

"At least, one more line from the above collection?"

"Let's do IT!"

("Two beautiful flirtatious sisters…" (NY: Simon and Schuster, 1988)

p.223 In

the very-Mean-Mean/time! I/I spoke about divorce, Italian style.
"..and what were we waiting for?" (…..too many W's?)

(Henry Miller, "The Cosmological Eye" (NY: New Directions, 1968) p.146

I WOULD GO

THAT WAY I

WOULD GO

THAT WAY

André Breton:"L'amour fou"

(Paris: Gallimard, coll. Metamorphosis, 1937)
"Now, I got my way

Now, I got my way"

Julius Lester, "Black Power's Gon "get your Mama" (NY: Grove Press, 1968) p.

80

("I see you weeping on your toes—to kiss—me from behind")
"Love Poems of Ancient Egypt," translated by Ezra Pound and Noel Stock
(NY: New Directions, 1962) p.14

I/I were dreaming of buying a Max Mara's Ornate Heeled Bootie, for only
$695.00, and a blue- Be-button down, and a bathing, from Sax, 70%, discount.

Brooks "Bro...   "OK for braces

for...$." "Then, I am your I..."
We speech rapidly

        "There is no language without
speech..."

Roland Barthes, "Elements of Semiology" translated by Annette Lavers and
Colin Smith (NY: Hill and Wang, 1967) p.15

THUS, VIOLON AND SOCIAL STUDIES...

Everything was a match, between Chinese porcelain, and Emily Dickenson
(translated into Frenchy, then, back into English.)

                                        ONE BY ONE

Everything was cleared away, by an insistent group of illegal Mexican
immigrants, singing their national anthem.

"Then,

An interroga-

tion

"Then, I'm

ready to go!"
Emily Dickenson: "Final Harvest" Poems selected and with an Introduction by
Thomas H. Johnson (NY: Little Brown, 1961) p. 42

In that huge conference room, everything was cleaned up, by an restive group
of illegal Mexicans, all of them who had managed to squeeze themselves,
through an imaginary wall.

As they broomed, they hymned, in unison, some revolutionary song.
Then, they could, so I thought, hear my answer:

"From then on, things moved quickly"

Norman S. Poser: [Escape] A Jewish Scandinavian Family, in the Second World
War" (NY: Sarreve Press, 2006) p.129

Besides all that talk, questions answered, looks of sadness, of happiness, of
squirming, waiting for one's turn...

A male, a self-acknowledged 18th century specialist, for relaxation, asked
around if anyone had ever read CANDIDE AND WHAT HAPPENED TO HER
WHEN SHE WAS SEARCHED FOR SECRETLY HIDDEN DIAMONDS?

("At least," answered a colonial specialist, those were fingers, prying into her
vagina, trying to reach, what turned out, to be a secret cache of diamonds, out
of Eldorado. (end of the anecdote.)

"All's wet! that ends   All's well!"

                                    But she did have to give up her Leica

As well as her green, original Olivetti

cover. (She did say she was terribly

ticklish.)
                    "Are you ticklish..."

(A linguist, a Saussurian, knew language WAS, as much a convention, as the
men's room, down the hall.)

"Ain't dat sumding?"

Now, All Stories are not equivalent to (of?) each other, or, at least, that's what some specialist might say.

"But it also had deep roots in the countryside"

"Anarchism from Theory to Practice" Daniel Guérin, with an Introduction by Naom Chomsky (NY: Monthly Review Press 1970) p. 119

And yet, with all those secret cameras concealed in her room, and, for example, in her chandelier, nothing she was doing or...I would even say, what she was planning to do, would be be registered.

She actually might have thought that her every page movement might attract the attention of some enemy reader and so, deliberately, she turned on a white page, and recited what she knew best:

"Les femmes doivent-elles participer un jour ā la vie politique ? OUI !

»

Georges Sand cried out.
                              I knew they knew.

"What's on the left side her bed?"

She held, in her hand, a Susan Sontag, New Testament.

                    I remembered a scene, seen at the Dragon...

(I never thought, not even for a minute, I'd be white-listed as a prospective

rapper!) On camera, she was caught scratching her lower back.
(Looked like a caryatide...pilloried onto a 19th century Blvd Raspail building.)

I had followed her, up her Toulouse staircase, five steps behind

her behind. I did catch a glimpse of her, in the third floor mirror.
          "There was something mysterious and smug in the way [she] spoke..."

          Ralph Ellison: "The Invisible Man" (NY: A signet Book, 1952) p.254

She had- indeed-- but my bosses, hidden, underneath Arlington Cemetery, had already seen that, as she climbed up her staircase, her skirt, flying up.

As she opened her door…

I caught sight of her bookcase:

There they were,

not quite the authors I had suspected I would see!

Hyppolyte Chaterion

Heine

Théodore Rousseau

Luigi Calamatta, and a reproduction of one of his expensive portraits

Agricol Perdi-

guyier De-

lacroix' Journal

Proudon

(Private Sex…)

Louis Viardot
Charles Fourier's material theories on communal love.

Louis Blanc and his Bois de Boulogne

George Sand and her Venice

(Gondoliring with Chopin…)

Mohammed Ennaji:"Serving the Master, Slavery and Society in
nineteenth century, Morocco" Translated by Seth Graebner (NY: St. Martin's

Press, 1998) p.91
She sounded, as she flushed her highly musical seat, like all of her thoughts
were emigrants, out of her books…

As she tried to rest, her mind tried to resolve a great problem:

"Why had those Protestants, in La Rochelle land, founded
a New Rochelle? Really, she mused, if they hadn't…then they would all have been
slaughtered by the king of France!

We walked through her town.

At least, those were her preliminary mumblings! And,
She was sure Moscow had captured all of her ambulating thoughts.

I did ask her, what was it like
To live in Toulouse?

And…had she ever visited that airplane factory, on one of those guided tours?

Her eyes
twinkled.
"We must now return to the problem of eroti-

cism…" (Why did my mind ever switch objects?)
Georges Bataille, "The Tears of Eros" translated by Peter Connor (The
John
Hopkins UP, 1989) p.83.

She turned to me, on Main Street, and asked me, if I loved oysters (sex,

centuries ago!) We ate them in a little Bistro.

(All bistros are "little"…)
(Was I doing my DC appoint-
ed job?)

I did ask her what she thought of Soviet activities in the
West.

For an answer, she recited lines of poetry Louise Michel had written, when she
got back from that future Dreyfus Island.

(I sent a secretly-CODED MESSAGE TO MY SUSPICIOUS SUPERIORS)

Talking about my own—and so far—unexplosive results, and I quoted one of
my most favorite philosophers:

"This endeavor, to bring it about, that our own likes and dislikes should meet
with universal applause."

Benedict Spinoza: "Ethics on the Understanding," Translated from the Latin
by R.H.M.Elwes (NY: Barnes and Noble Books, 2000) p.83.

(I wondered (if-- all to myself-- If she had actually read any of Rosa Luxembourg's

writings?)

She did say,

Eating her last oyster, that women spies, looked great in Hollywood movies. We

got to her place (I already knew her staircase!)

In my barely concealed desire, I asked her to put on her old pyja-

mas. I did ask her, if she believed all spies had to be cremated?

Emily Dickenson:

A

word

is

dead

When

it is

said

Some

say

A smell of cooking.

She said,

"My Young brother so wanted to learn how to play the violin!"

He played, with her left nipple.

He sobbed. She smiled.
She said:

    "Can you imagine him, throwing away his violin, just because of his
    teacher's hand…?"

We performed what all couples in, and out, of movies did, when they were on
a bed, anywhere in the world, including Toulouse.

We fucked.

Then, I/I put on clean sheets.

(Now, sweaty and sticky-white)

She noted, and then, she said:

"Your testicles now look like one of Pasteur's experiments!"

Then, an

ACT

(I'M STARVING!)

"For what?"
"Cinese"

"For What?" I inquired...

"D2

CWG SF11

SS10"

She said: "Free delivery! Cookies included. Chop sticks included. White paper

napkins included."

And yet:

"She didn't touch a thing,

She kept him at a distance."

Elena Ferrante, "My Brilliant Friend" translated from the Italian by Ann Goldstein
(NY: Europa Editions, 2014) p.227

"strangers
"On a train?"
(Hummed)

I asked her, as we chopped-sticked into SS10, if she liked to talk to...

She smiled:

"Only when I'm not working."

In the meantime, I saw a map of France, on her kitchen wall, and, a red needle
stuck into...Toulouse.

I played with my memory, so far, full of steam and...so, I tried, and succeeded, remembering all the books on her shelves.

Then I whispered to myself:

"that's
ough!"

"But to me, this experiment doesn't seem contrived." (Eric Rhodes, "Speculations on the Cinema" (NY: Chilton Books, 1967) p. 166.

It's always a question of something,
As I went about my CIA search for guilt activities...

I always wanted a quote from Jane Gardam, "Old Filth," but, that was only a fleeting temptation.

(I'm sure she was totally unaware that I carried, right above my ankle, a receptor of everything we were saying. Besides, everything we were doing, and saying, was instantaneously recorded by that camera, and, by the listening device, placed in her chandelier.

I stared at her, and her priceless radio:

a Zenith 60317, NY: World's Fair, 1939

She really had a real gorgeous other radio:

A Detroit 146E, 1938

"Boy," I said to myself,   "I'd give my right loyal-

ty for those two jewels!"
I later found out, well-- a couple of weeks later-- in the attic, where she communicated with her Soviet patrons, by speaking into her two radios!

"Where had she gotten all those

priceless ob-

jects? "   All my grandfather's,
In his military trunk, I found jewelry from his grandmother's, letters of love, and condolencences, written to a corporal, in a trench, next to mine. In a hell hole, I found German medals, a German rifle, a copy of Céline's "Voyage au bout de la nuit." A letter, indicating where he wanted to be buried and, next to whom, and what he wanted to be written on his tombstone. I found the deed to his

town house, in the XV1 arrondissement, and lots more in another trunk!"

"So?"

"I sold them all!, including. the XV1 arrondissement town house, all of that, to a wealthy Russian magnet, who had already purchased a property in Antibes."

"All of that?   "We sold! All of that!"

"Godwin explored the relationship between subject and master."

Ronald Paulson, "Representations of Revolution (1789-1820)" (New Haven and London: Yale University Press, 1983) p.231

>   I thought to myself, now—
>   "there's a family member, living reality!"

By chance (but, in reality, chance hardly ever exists) I think, I really, hardly existed as an autonomous individual, now, that I've signed up with CIA, headquartered below Arlington cemetery.

I asked her if I could hang up my wet raincoat in her

closet.

>   "Over there."

She took out a wooden hangar and, put my wet coat on it.

I caught sight, in her closet, what her chandelier had already seen:

>   A blue outfit.

Blue sandals.

A blue broom

stick. Now I sus-

pected I knew!
She'd dress in that outfit,
Entered that Toulouse laboratory,

And, with her broom stick, photographed anything left on all the desks, by lunching, hungry scientists, cutting up a steak, pommes frites and a glass of (cheap) red wine from Australia.

(Our chandelier camera could also record our conversations and, in a second, place that info

On my boss's desk.)

And yet, I had that haunting thought, that, within a week, she'd be sending her recently photographed material, back to Moscow's HQ, below Lenin's tomb, Cold As Hell, in the winter.

"On the other hand:

Whereby the body did all the writing"

T. Thilleman, "Blasted Tower" (Charleston, SC, 2004) p.187

CIA did know that, before we ever caught sight of her, of her Soviet activities, she had, as a young lycée

Student played an awful lot of Chopin's Venice compositions.
                              By chance, in Venice,
That may have been... her first contact with classical Soviet music? Even, perhaps, that had influenced her.

987424 social studies teacher?

He did say, sometimes, in private, to one of his best students, after his office hours, that he did find post-war Soviet materialism quite attractive.

                              A   waltz

Played Chopin

One early afternoon, the principal left the building, to smoke one of her Camel cigarettes.

Then, she heard him play, on an old, decrepit, up-

right. "I guess," she said, to both of us, she really

appreciated Chopin!"
She thought to herself, as you were dozing off, head on the keyboard, I thought I heard you mumbling something about Moscow!

He wanted to know if she had ever wished to stand, looking at Lenin's tomb, on a snowy day.

He mused.
Did he ever listen to my musings?

> Once again, Emily Dicken-
>
> son, "Those fair—
>
> fictitious People The
>
> women"

She did imagine what he was thinking, at that very second, and she said:

"out loud"…

> Still, room enough, next to her keyboard, for sex…

sex!"

He was convinced that she was always able to project her

thoughts. Once again, the same Dickenson:

> "A
> word is
> dead

> When it is

said…"

(Too much of a truth to be written down.)

> "What about
> pasta?"

Freed of all desires for a Soviet decipher, I decided to purchase, for dinner, a most expensive Bordeaux 1932.

Anyone, with an ounce of desire, would stand by the hot water, waiting for it

to boil.

> " Swivel the sauce with a wooden spoon."

For some difficulty, I wondered why I was thinking of Chinese noodles, on a Chinese New Year,

when, from nearly every store and building, giant rotating fire crackers machine, lightened up the pavement, with all sorts of colors, especially red ones.

We sat down at her kitchen table.

We ate.

We wiped our tomato sauce off our chins.

                  "Do you

have the   slightest idea about

what should we do with all those home-

less on

Broadway?

               (She had, recently, read all about them, in the Ruska Soviet
Newspaper, with a Tarzan comic sequence, at the bottom of that paper's
front page.

Then, she turned to me, and said:
"Aren't you one of those filthy US capitalists?"

 Then, she added:

               "Go on with your merdy dissertation!"
"I need it to land a job!"

("That was a real commy statement," he said, under his breath,

even though her intonation hadn't changed a lot.)

Then, in her now openly working voice, she said: "Get the fuck
out of my life, you filthy capitalist..."

(no sauce left.)

Did she know we had thrown out the window, our senator, for his tyrannical
interrogations views?)

1) I sent all that back to my superiors, thinking that the sauce might have
jumbled our truths.

2) All of that, having been preceded by a quote from the "CRM: The Journal of
Heritage Stewardship" (Winter, 2010)

3) All of that, probably due to the spreading of Hegel, in an existential
interpretation, a serious ideological challenge to Marxism.

For the time being, not a further peep from my Toulouse bedroom and...my oysters (they say it's a very old sex ...success.)

I took a TGV to Paris

"Look!"

As a kid looks out a

window: Cows
Sheep

A small church

A small village

A field, with gushing water flowing over it.

..."He would never be left out with the rain. Doesn't that explain everythi

ng?"   Gary Snyder, "Left out in the rain" (San Francisco:

North Point Press, 1986) p. 17
In Paris, I joined my CIA buddy, humming an American tune, in Apollinaire square, checking out the Figaro, for a movie called "The Dragon Lady."

     As a reminder, I said:

       "Any news on the Paris Commie front?"
 "Was Maurice Thorez, a real " sodomightY?'
"I know, you were able to follow her every footstep, with your ankle-high

recording machine! You know what I mean! In the métro, on the bus, in an

Uber taxi...

        "Anywhere OUT OF this dark

world!!" We took a bus to Butte Chaumont.
I truly wanted a break!

      (Too many exclamation marks?)

"Know any good cafés? That coffee was only, half-

way, drinkable.
99

Cars passed us by....

(How I wish I knew her real name!)

I truly hoped she'd ask me the same question...

In a muffled voice, on my portable, I said, one day, I'd return to my previous self,
as if I had been mounted by a voudoo LOA!"

"Enough   of

all that   fabrica-

tion! Like a ballet.
It said, in a mechanical voice:
                              " Now..."

In bed, on the third floor, she reminded me of a Boucher

painting. (Nothing like art, to switch gears.)
I dreamt of owning 2 cars:

                              1959 BMW 507
                              series and...A

1958 Rolls Royce Silver Cloud, drop head

In the meantime, I felt something wetting our bed.
 A NY Times, January 11, 2015, main section, or at least, that's the way I JUSTIFIED
 it!
                    "IT Had a logical FEEL TO IT."

Marcel Duchamp: "Paris Notes" (Paris: Centre national d'art...) n.d. p.69

When all WAS said, and neatly done, I followed her to what was supposed to be
a highly secret location, of the French CP.

                    (Deconstruction, via Lacan...)
My photographic equipment saw her take out a fancy key.
            (Her heels allowed me to follow her every footstep.)

Above the elevator door, you could read the fol-

                              lowing:

"Desire

Dyna-

mo!"

(Marcel Duchamp, ibid … num-

bert 161.) Too tight! She took off

her left high heel.

Now,
she took off her other high heel, as if she suspected someone might be following
her every footsteps.

She fancied an elegant elevator, with a cushioned bench, and a floor-to-ceiling

mirror! She did have a recurring dream that, one day, she'd find, in a hedge, a

newborn.
                    "The other day besides a hedge

                    I found a low-born shepherdess…"

Lawrence Venuti, "The Translator's Invisibility" (NY: Routledge, 1995)

p.229

                    "Hello" she said.
               And… "How are YOU?"
He asked, with an intonated intonation.

Too timid to answer, but, as she sat down, in front of his ornate desk, probably
a throw-away 18th century one, after 1789.
She admired a recently painted portrait of Marx and Engels.

               Here's another
               Piece of Prose

Together, with (a) Lenin, nearly washed out by Leni Reifenstahl, and, another, still
a half--size Stalin, smiling, somewhere in a fake countryside.
   She had been warned that, it was possible, that a hidden CIA agent might be
totally able to catch……. her every word, her every movement, such as crossing
her legs, for instance, or taking off her Cartier watch (a Chinese imitation, sold in
lots of fine Bolzanop stores, and on the street of Venice)
101

She opened her expensive, leather Saint Laurent bag, and, wiped a speck of dust

off her nose. A drizzle. HE mulled over an unanswerable thought:

"Could she be a CIA agent?"

In her secret ear phone, she heard:

"Anything else to report?"

"She wondered if, all of that was True?"
Dan Pope, "House-Breaking" (NY: Simon and Schuster, 2015) p.87

As a pseudo. CP journalist, for L'Humanité, she might have suspected that a CIA agent followed her every footstep, look, and, desire lock, stock and barrrrel!

Toulouse warned her that her every move might be taped and sent to

DC.   "Be

very careful!"

She hushed.
One of the guards, off duty, stopped, in a doorway, and started to talk to himself.

"When will vacation come?"

He was mulling over his first cook-out.

One uttered to another,
"Who gives a damn!"

She suspected they might be following her, by someone, still unresolved.
He hid behind an oak, facing CP Headquarters, and jotted down her every word,
every gesture. (My equipment was in perfect harmony with what it was manufactured to do.)

"According to this pseudo-Aristotelian tradition, the personality of the subject can be grasped through the precise interpretation of somatic clues..."

Richard Brilliant, "Wanted $2000 reward" (London: Reaktion Books, 2008) p. 76

"How could daddy, now overseas, doing his official job, ever figure that one out!"

Inexplicably, the scene switched to an "Elsewhere," as far away as thinkable, from Paris, or, for that matter, from daddy's good paying job, to his retirement benefits.

Was I remembering something like a "past," or were all those beers, cutting into my memory?

"Actually, they were celebrating my

birthday!"

(I hated birthdays: they all reminded

me of death.)

My French-Soviet spy!

But nothing could rival my CIA mission, but, to follow...

My dream was doing the same

thing on Holloweeen..

All of a sudden,
And...   all of that.

"Based, on a large part, on the result of as personal research..."

Jack Yeager, "The Vietnamese novel written in French" (Hanover and London: 1987) p.166.

She was going to the bathroom, and said she'd be back, in a second or two.
She disappeared.

I bought Le Monde.

Checked out American tourists , ALL AROUND ME, AT THE 2 Magots

Holding, in their sweaty hands, a bilingual dictionary

"Mercy, boocoop"
One black musician, a contemporary of Josephine Baker, asked what someone might like to hear

On the clarinette he had played, in that famous Bal Nègre.

Somebody, probably an American scholar, researching Peggy Guggenheim, for a documentary, went bananas, when he went to her palatial museum, in Venice, where Peggy had amassed a huge art collection of surrealist paintings.

"The new art of color, the writing of Robert and Sonia Delaunay" Arthur A. Cohen. (NY: The Viking Press, 1978) p.45.

I whispered, to myself, how great it would have been, as a Ph'in deed, my way through my Social Studies, rather than allowing me to paint on the floor.

My name's still, Cohen...

NAPOLEON, himself, gave Jews lots of recognition. I might have been there, in his empire, waiting for the good news!

"To the very end of the ancient régime, the rabbinate of the region, and especially of the city of Metz, was quite distinguished."

Arthur Hertzberg, "The French Enlightenment and the origins of Modern anti-

semitism." (NY: Schocken books, 1968) p.166.
I mulled over my secret desire, to ask her, to towel my back.
            I told her, I would do the same, when she stepped out of her bath.

See "Tonks," in "Harry Potter, A Sticker Collection" (San Rafael, CA, n. d) n. p.

("Did I ever tell you, (a repetition) that New Rochelle was founded to increase test results for our failing high school kids,in La Rochelle?)

At times, everything I had been asked to perform vanished in an oyster

shell,

with heaven on top?

Francis Ponge, "Le parti pris des choses" (Paris: Poésie, 1967)p. 42

After all, spies are not made up every day and...working for Washington

D. C!A.
I remembered a short story I thought I might write, someday, to entertain my future kids,
That, as a secret face, I could flush out some tidbits, and rise above being a Paris-bound spy, checking out how that young woman I was following, and, had

followed to the Soviet Embassy, would be equally trained, as Toulouse had been...

I even played with a quote about her, to pass the time of a late

afternoon!

"Where can a woman get the money to save in any other busi-

ness?"

George Bernard Shaw, "PLAYS" (NY: Herbert Stone, 1898) p.203

A paid Soviet spy, just like me, in CIA, below a Cemetery!

"The brevity of the preceding remarks can be remedied, to some extent, by dwelling somewhat longer..."

Jean Piaget (Structuralism) Translated and edited by Chaninah Moscher (NY: Harpers Torchbooks, 1970) p.106

Now a poem

Yo
u
I

stared

a
t
h
er

TURN THE PAGE

Hair

Quick

No
here

As if I could decipher the meaning of her Being,...

HER

Words, even written, never gave up the totality of meanings.

If she were, in actuality, a spy for the Soviets, beneath Lenin's tomb, then her solution was right around the corner of Blvd St. Germain, and the medical school.

From there, she could easily walk to the Luxembourg Gardens, and, see kids pushing little one-sail boats, with a wooden stick.

She sat down, at an inviting outdoor café.

I dreamt, in a public space, probably unsuspected by my bosses, that I, too, would sit on one of those chairs, sipping uninteresting coffee.

I saw her reading an afternoon paper.

(AS I WAS TO FOLLOW HER (let's put that, right here, in

(CAPS)

I began,
rapidly Thinking

The impossible.

A Paris-So-

viet spy?

Would

that have happened to someone else, crossing the gardens?

He spoke into his discreet mike,

"Did that ever happen to you, in

Toulouse?"

He added

"Did I ever follow her to her digs?"

"Have you ever been softened by what you have seen/

lived?" (I remember dreaming that one thing never displaced another.)
Then, I added, what was probably equally applicable to my own duties:

One bed (does not make

love, by itself.)

Another! (Dream ...?)

In fact,

one dream never displaces an...
In fact, has your dream ever occurred in
your walking hours?

"Do not sweat it!"
(One agent, always displaces another!)
(it is a secret.)
As of that moment, in the hiring hall, in that hotel, when both of us were swept
up by the CIA, both of us have been true friends, especially sent to the same
country! Toulouse and...Paris!

"Who could ask for anything more?"

"Why not envisage a
Bundie- to-body experience?

I mean, the four of us, somewhere on a nudie beach,
Somewhere, in the south of France."

"Body to bodies?"

"And, for starters, on any warm afternoon, lying on a large towel, with the Eifel

Tower on it, We could begin, by reading a horrible event, in the Soviet Union,
with prisoners, like us, in a 19thcentury Siberian salt mine."

"How's that, for starters?" AND I WHISPERED:
"Who would ever have suspected that, in our cherished peace-time, 2 Americans
were to be convicted to years of slave labor, somewhere in an unknown
geography?"

"Fuck off!"

"That's no way to end a wonderful holiday-stay, in Toulouse or
Paris!"

"I say, when the body
speaks..."
(No applicable quote, here.)
107

"And yet, when we speak, we should remember the

"Song of Solomon"

section 2:

"O that you would kiss me with the kisses of your mouth!"
(Have you ever counted them?)

"Life's too short to start counting!"

"Or, would you testify that, in a dream, even an Egyptian one, surrounded by
Egyptian statuettes, you could really be counted in a working half-asleep prose?"

("I've got to admit, that, even, in a walking prose, so much there is in absolute
need of clarification? Did our future Soviet questioners ever hold a Freudian
Bible?")

"Would they ever skip prose, and require dream

poem?

"Whatever..."

I replied.
"Ok! My suppositions wobbled in prose!"

For a second, in the interrogation room, answers were side-swiped into a corner.
I'd think, in my own secret mental room...

"Not enough sun-
light, here!"

(I whispered to myself:
("did anyone ever listen, when this sort of a talking cure, or rather, a running
sentence of hypotheses. ever occur?")

The difficulty was audible: for I/I had a tendency of shuffling words.

"I lay upon a grave or bed."
Elizabeth Bishop, "The Complete Poems" (NY: Farrar, Straus and Giroux, 1969)
p.22

Over both of their speaking machines (still on their ankle socks) D.C. caught every

syllable to void meaning,

I implanted a memory.

....

Then, I said, in half a whisper,

"When would their worn-out words take flight?"

(I smelled the kitchen of a Siberian kitch-

en:

tongues, ears, fingers, toes...)

An
audible
sound

My stomach gurgles:

The mind-movie showed a Florida beach, with gorgeous Russian babes, sun-
tanning and...pushing Soviet hands off their bodies!

They unplugged our ears.

"Now, you can verbally dream!"

I asked myself, when does the end really

End?

End? (There we were!)

(Talking a km a minute!)

I turned a CIA-album, with the I/I of us photographed, and
asked weird questions:

"Like, can the body go beyond Meaning, or could there be
a wrong syntax of meaning?"

I answered, for both of US/ ONE, as we left that Washington Hotel, to become
ONE, as both of us, wished to be ONE.

(For a short time of being: One equaled Two, as words follow gestures...)

Both of us ONE, WONDERED IF I/I had, as of an unsuspected Being, linked
Meaning to meaning...

"The Division of the terrain..."
(Walter S. Gibbon: "Breugel" (NY: Oxford UP, 1977)p. 29

My own logic forced me to reconsider the concept of a "Blizzard" of meaning, or, to put it in another mode of writing:

"I don't mind remembering..."

(Eugene O'Neil, "The Great..." (NY: Brown: "The Fountain, The Moon of the Caribbean" 1926) p.79

I turned to a photo of both of us, looking at our: "selves," in a 42nd Street distorting mirror.

Was I only a noun?
                    "Something hiding its selves?"

To make sense of what had happened, I uttered to myself:
                                        "When does the End End?"

I wanted to know, if you knew when knowledge was an obstructing necessity?

                                        A 1960's Happening
More, before I touch an answer.
Perhaps, I tried to find out, before mourning clarity.

(One fact, we held, commonly, in our mouth, was how to disregard how we tended to munch on words.)

Her voice (s)

            A response   without words

She stared, ahead, and said:
                    "You're the best lover, so far..."

Naked,
            On a nudie beach, we: I/I found it flattering.

Had
            our umbrella, like her window, stayed shuttered?

            (Rather, could one touch each other, and utter:

                    "Ding und Sich?)

                    We heard a train whistle.

(Somebody, still on Platform A, wondered where could that train have gone?)
A shadow shot.

(Fritz Lang's?)

She held, in her left hand, her keys and a copy of

Paul Nizan
"Aden Arabie"

Translated by Joan Pinkham, from the French (NY: Monthly Review Press, 1968)
p. 75.

She nearly fell out of meaning.

"Now, Moscow might give me a medal: Gold? Silver?
Bronze? For all that secret information I had sent?"

O! Happiness!
Truth!
I touched her key

I uttered, in half a breath, that key, now, is mine!

In her half-ritualized voice
She remembered Voltaire:
"A prejudice has long been entertained, in the Russian Church, that it is not
lawful to say mass without testicles…"

Voltaire, "Satirical Dictionary" (NY: Mount Vernon Press, 1946) p. 112

In the meantime, I, too, took a sniff of her elegant perfume, out of a Baudelaire
poem, out of the top drawer of her dresser.

(Should I invoke my Toulouse flat?)

Even at home (where else?) she had all her dresses cleaned, in a local laundry,
and hand- delivered.

"Strikes in Detroit"

She said: "Is that the penultimate end of capitalism?"

L'Humanité's. front page, in Caps,

HUGE LETTERS

The End is...

It's Coming

She believed that, based on her religious education, similar to Emma Bovary's,

She said to herself:
"Let proper authorities lubricate that belief."

(She kept her eye open, just as Bunùel had sought)

During that intermission, Toulouse, in that late afternoon, in bed, with the shutters half-closed,
Sprayed whipped cream on her Toulouse Lautrec.

In the foreground, her ears:

Keith Jarrett, playing one of his greatest in Berlin.

Audaciously, she added to her imaginary colleague

An American special: "Let's do it!"

Then I licked her sweat.

Hoagy Carmichael, playing the keys in "Casablanca"

She blew out the dust, off the needle, while the airplane swept him away to
Freedom

"Our consciousness," says Husserl, "is always CONSCIOUSNESS of something"

"The Philosophy of Edmund Husserl" (NY: Anchor Books, 1967) p.377

(Is there anybody here, who can contradict that?)

She loved bouncing off me, especially when I leaned on her right side.

A ceiling mirror played its composition.

"We huddled
We cuddled"
            Paris murmured.

("Was it really the truth that my company had to take an elevator to get us below some cemetery?")

"Did I have to do my duty, in order to wire Moscow?"

Anything, to purify our Republic.

At that instant, she came up with a quote:

      Sam Swope: "I am a pencil, a Teacher, His Kids, and the world of stories." (NY: Henry Holt, 2004) front cover.

That's what a mother may have wanted to express.

We were chosen to be together, in this world.

      "I'm looking right and left to see if anybody is looking."

William Carlos Williams, "Paterson" (NY: New Directions, 1937) p.209

"Take it from me, I'm a twin of myself."

"Focus on your hand"
                Another poem
                    Her back
                    Her back

"HOWEVER, those words were addressed only to me."

Thomas Bernhard, "Woodcutters" (Chicago UP, 1987)p. 134

Then a smile
A statement:
   "I've been doing that, all along!"

                 "Gotta"
Jumps out of her bed.

The other, stretches his arm.
          "Now
I'm all alone!

            Whoopie!"

           "Who are you, really?"

Toulouse and Paris, early ALONE,

                        "Listen:
                        I'm naked!"
                        "I'm naked!"
Internet dialogue.
At home, we call that:

                        Screwing around and around, as if we were in a
                        1952 Buick.

"Would you ever suspect, that the teachers, in the auditorium, were rehearsing:
                        "Ballads for Americans?"

In fact, the Violin turned into a kid's sail boat.

                        The class nazellyed.

She said:
                        "Do you realize what's happening to the Left in our country?"

She sat, on the edge of her desk.

Social Studies asked, all of us,
                        "if our parents had ever evoked the 30's in the US?"

She so admired:
                        John Stewart Curry!
And then she added:
                        "New Masses"

"Did your parents know that Louis Zukofsky had once written for that magazine?"

This is what John R. Searl was to write, in his SPEECH ACTS (Cambridge UP 1977)
p.62.

                        "Insincere promises"

"You can tell your parents, that's the truth about American lies!"

Then, she uncrossed her silk stockings legs, and cried, in her box of Kleenex.

                        She wrote out her declamatory poem.

            "Our   France

Was once
The Enlightenment"

(To hell with Mme Bovary's priest.)

(Some 18th century nobleman said, under his perfumed breath:

"I must find a virgin, around here, about to get married.

"A Virgin."   (An opera...?)

In the meantime, why don't you check out Plato's "The Collected Dialogues,
including the letters, edited by Edith Hamilton and Huntington Carnes (Princeton:
Bollingen Series, LXX1) p. 124

"Stop tickling!"

"All power to US!"
Somebody added:

"Head-chopping will get you no—where!"

(The teacher, and our wishful legs)

In the back of the second floor classroom, girls in the back, passed to the ones in
the front, a secret message.
The former social studies instructor entertained one of his long gone secrets.

"Stop tickling"

She whispered to herself, looking at herself in a mirror, of her own invention.

The bell rang twice

He heard himself say, out- loud:

"To the nearest Athenian Bar"

(What the "diable" is a tradition, if you don't excuse it?)

In a cellar, still visible, a portable type writer
with hardly a key, a green cover, dirtied, by fallen
Glass, piercing it.

An old, impossible to identify, typewriter. On the roller, half a page burned-out.

The novelist, staring at a pile of debris, said: "That's a fine opener."

The night was darker than usual, and he said: "Twinkle…"

Out of the rubble:
A graduation picture
Boys in blue
(Girls doing what girls do, for an official school picture.
Teeth, wide open… etc.)

NEXT DAY, SAME THING

Samuel Beckett, "Waiting for Godot" (NY: Evergreen Press, 1982) p.36

(Estragon)

Mother read us the conductor's letter.

"They found themselves, pitchforked"

George Orwell, "Coming up for Air" (NY: Harcourt, Brace and co., 1950) p.119

(The conductor, in a sing-song manner (as in a Brecht.)

"They'll be fed correctly. Housed correctly, clothed correctly."

A signature.

He refused to add precisions:
Now, he knew

The smell…
In fact, he added:
"All's well…"

He said to himself, how could he ever forget, what his eyes had seen, not so far ahead, with huge chimneys, smoking.

To clean out that smell, he remembered, now years ago, that, at an Easter campfire, wood burned and smoke flew all around.

Then, he took a shot of a poor red wine, and added, silently:

"All's well that begins well!"

(Lyrics, all around a piano solo.)

They call them hot dogs, as the novelist reminded us.

"We'll dance, at your wedding!"

(Somebody had, a long, long time ago, read about a Bovary wedding feast.)

The philosophy teacher tried to remember a metaphysical answer...
Nothing doin!

it's where I want to go, after this affair:

> Beijing
> Shanghai (despite the awful stink)
> Shijiazhuang
> X' an
> Hong Kong (that reminded her of a
> Hollywood mobie)
> Tianjin
> Kunming
> Hangzhou

(A visa..
An up-to-date passport picture, medical test results...and off
she'd go!

She got to the point, having seen lots and lots of pictures of China, that she began seeing Chinese in her dreams.

"What a boring sing-song all that had been."

She sing-songed a murmur

"Going to school, in Toulouse!"

She thought, further on, as a Soviet spy, would her vegetarian superiors ever let her leave France to frequent another language?

As it is said:
"Her mouth watered with desires..."

To calm her hopes, she found a way of forgetting Toulouse, by learning Provençal, and listening to troubadours make their loves known, together, on a stringed instrument!

I folded my mental umbrella, and said to myself,
"I'll never wear blue again!

Our black-robed priest, reminded all of us women, not to forget, our Thursday meetings.

His voice rose, as he approached the end of his thought.

"That Red Ball Express!"

"Where did all that come into being?"

He walked back to his apt.
He nearly forgot to bless us all,

"Bless you, all!"

He said,

Raising his right hand, above his head.

Mme Fleur seemed to see the American novelist, spreading his legs, apart, as he sat, near a non-working chimney.

On a cot, his neighbor had loaned him and, which allowed him to see his local Street.
He put a pillow over his eyes and…tried to fall asleep.

"Human story is told, it can be likened to a circularity."
T. Thilman. The special body (NY: Rain Mountain Press, 2016) p.233

But he heard, then he looked out his dirty window, and saw Adults, rifles shouldered
And all holding shovels.

They sang the Marseillaise.
A large group of middle-aged women sang the "International"

In a chorus, they sang:
"Death to the conductor!"
"Suicide is not good enough!"

They entered the winter-bound cemetery, and walked to the conductor's grave.

With their shovels, they disinterred the coffin.
They placed him against the cemetery gates, and shot him a second death.

\

The body was nearly decomposed.
It didn't stop the men who took the remains and, in the town square, they tied
what remained of the body to the old oak tree.

The wowen applauded.
There, they pelted the remains, with little stones, picked up along the way.

In the morning, what remained was swept up by the town's sanitation team.

Then, the women, walking back to town, in a chorus, recited a well-known page
from the Kabbala, and they rewrote it:

"Since there was evil desire and a serpent..."

The women sang in unison.

Gershom Scholem, "On the Kabbalah and Its Symbolism." (NY: Schocken Books,
1977) p. 79, for the original.

The body had turned to dust.
Now, they asked in a chorus:
"And where will we put the remains, now?"

The men could hear, one of the older citizens saying:

"Soon they'll have no more space for my coffin!"
The American novelist said he heard somebody say:

"This was all just too much for him to process."

Loren Long and Phil Bildner, "Books for your years." (NY: Simon and Schuster 2007)
p.71.

All acknowledged:

"Much of what is to come is hidden..."

Ossip Mandelstam, "Selected Poems" a bilingual edition, translated by David
McDuff (NY: Farrar Strauss and Giroux, 1975)p.147

Then he added:

"That's life!"

They touched each other, and whispered in each one's ear:
"I don't get it!"

Again, both uttered in unison, nearly secretly, in the back of an imaginary Sorbonne classroom:

"Metaphysics comes in late afternoon!"

Then, both future philosophy lycée teachers, and, in a CHORUS, said:

"In fact, what is the real Meaning of meaning?"

"Move your hand more to the right."

Finally, he thought:

No more Fourier
No more Bakunin

Now, near the end:

No Metalanguage
No Intertextualities

THEN THE END

And then, we now know, he looked at that piece of paper and said:

"In return, I signed the agreement of the sale..."

Daniel Defoe, "Robinson Crusoe" (NY: Signet Classics, 2008)p. 69

ADD

"And so suggestive of a design to delude the beholder..."
Sherman Cody, "The Best Tales of Edgar Allan Poe" (Chicago: A.C McLurg and Company, MCMXVII)

A Self Definition (by the author)

I was born in Paris and docked in Manhattan.

Upon arrival, Mrs. Kaufman taught me English in PS 54. Thereafter, probably due to my French accent, my sis and I were given full scholarships to attend the Bentley School. After my graduation, entered Columbia College and graduated in 1954. Then my dear neighbors sent me to Korea, where I remained for 18 months, managing to visit Thailand, Cambodia, India, and, for some great meals, Hong Kong.

Thereafter, my CC, MA, and Ph.D.,   all from Columbia. I was then hired by the French department at Barnard College. After a number of years, became chair, and retired 50 years later.

During the following years, I received a Guggenheim and an NEH, as well as two awards from the French government!.

My poetry in French was first published in Paris in 1961: *Lectures et compte-rendu* (POL).

I was then published by 23 small presses (*Al Dante, La Souteraine, Ulysses-fin-de-siecle,* and many others.

My poetry in magazines (always in French: *Les temps modernes, Tel quel, Action poétique, Banana Split,* and many others.

Then, my first book of poetry in Eglish: *Sixty-six for starters* (Jensen)

Among other full length translations, of *2 Francis Ponge* (UCP,) *Six Contemporary French Women Poets* (U of Southern Ill UP), *Joyce Mansour* (Black Widow press) and Louis Zukofsky's *Guillaume Apollinaire* (Weslyan UP)

Finally, together with my co-translator, Francois Dominique, the whole of Louis Zukofsky's *"A."*

I am now working on my fifth novel: *Charbovary.*

About CHAX

Founded in 1984 in Tucson, Arizona, Chax has published 200 books in a variety of formats, including hand printed letterpress books and chapbooks, hybrid chapbooks, book arts editions, and trade paperback editions such as the book you are holding. In August 2014 Chax moved to Victoria,Texas, and is presently located in the University of Houston-Victoria Center for the Arts, which has generously supported the publication of *At Night on the Sun*, which has also received support from many friends of the press. Chax is an independent 501(c)(3) organization which depends on support from various government and private funders, and, primarily, from individual donors and readers.

Recent and books include *The Complete Light Poems*, by Jackson Mac Low, *Life–list*, by Jessica Smith, *Andalusia*, by Susan Thackrey, *Diesel Hand*, by Nico Vassilakis, *Dark Ladies*, by Steve Mc-Caffery, *What We Do*, by Michael Gottlieb, *Limerence*, by Saba Razvi, *Short Course*, by Ted Greenwald and Charles Bernstein, *An Intermittent Music*, by Ted Pearson, *Arrive on Wave*, by Gil Ott, *Entangled Bank*, by James Sherry, *Autocinema*, by Gaspar Orozco, *The Letters of Carla, the letter b.*, by Benjamin Hollander, *A Mere Ica*, by Linh Dinh, *Visible Instruments*, by Michael Kelleher, *Diesel Hand* (letterpress), by Nico Vassilakis, and *At Night on the Sun*, by Will Alexander, and *The Hindrances of Householders*, by Jennifer Bartlett.

You may find CHAX online at *https://chax.org*